Charlotte Byrne

Other stories by Charlotter Byrne:

In Which Dragons are Real But 2018
9780992858162

First Came Fear: New Tales of Horror
9780997264920

The Collection: Flash Fiction for Flash Memory
9780692991039

Purple Lights
9780992858131

Folked Up

Crystal Peake Publisher
www.crystalpeake.co.uk

First edition published in March 2020 by Crystal Peake
Publisher

Print I S B N 978-1-912948-16-1
eBook I S B N 978-1-912948-17-8

Typeset by Crystal Peake Publisher
Cover designed by Fuyu Dust

Visit www.crystalpeake.co.uk for any further information.

For everyone who believed I could, but especially for my ridiculous family. Cheers!

1

Matty

If the world had an arsehole, I reckon Usher's Well would be it. It's not that it's a terrible place, it's just so bloody awkward to get to. Even more so when you're driving a temperamental old Morris Traveller that's low on petrol, the weather's not great and the heater's broken and you're shitting yourself in case you get pulled over because you only have a provisional license.

The village is tucked away in deepest, darkest Kent. Sandy's spent most of her time as navigator with her feet up on the dashboard and her nose stuck in some dog-eared road atlas that used to be her granddad's. She's not just interested in vintage, she's a bloody anachronism. I often wonder why she can't just be normal and like normal stuff and do normal things. It'd make birthdays easier for one thing.

'It can't be far now,' she says, squinting at the squiggly lines. 'It's meant to be just past Ashford.'

'Oh, yeah?' I snort. 'And where's that? You've brought us off the beaten track.'

She sniffs triumphantly and then whacks me with the atlas.

'Next left, Smart-arse. Want a sweet?'

I nod, and she pops a wine gum in my mouth as I stick the indicator on. We turn into what looks like a dirt track. I have my doubts as the car jigs up and down over pothole central, our instruments bang about in the back, and I nearly choke on the sweet. Trees hunch over and block out most of the grey sky. Some leaves brush against the windows and I'm just about to shoot my mouth off when I spot it.

However hard it was to find, I'm guessing it's hard to get lost in this village. The green itself is one massive roundabout with a maypole stuck dead in the centre, presumably ready for the festivities next week. The buildings are lined up all around it. It's laughable. Everything looks like it should have been knocked down years ago.

'So, where's this gaff we're playing at?' I mouth it quietly at Sandy. A few of the locals are beginning to stare, but that's probably because of a strange car on their turf. I can feel curtains twitching, and it's making me uneasy.

'Go up there.' Sandy waves at a cobbled path between the barber's and the post office. I'm guessing it's meant to be a road. We twist and turn past a few more dead houses until we reach a gravel drive. At the end of it is what looks more like a witch's cottage from a fairy tale than a pub, but there's a weather-beaten sign swinging from rusted hinges telling us we're in the right place. The Jack-in-the-Green Inn is the first stop on our tour. It starts to spit as we park up, and we give ourselves a chuffed high five before running inside.

Even if the village is horror story territory, this pub seems all right despite the heat. They've got a fire going in the hearth at one end, and even the furniture seems to be sweating. It's decked out olde-worlde style, with wooden beams and horse brasses everywhere, and some music from the year dot is playing. I think "cosy" is the word you use to describe places like this. Even the woman behind the bar looks like she could be your aunt. She's busy shuffling cardboard displays of pork scratchings but turns as Sandy and I approach.

'The Groveses, isn't it?' Her face lights up and she starts talking to Sandy like she's known her for years. Who knows, perhaps she has – Sandy was desperate to come here, for whatever reason. Said she had a feeling about the place.

The woman squawks and shakes my hand a bit too hard.

'It's lovely to have some young blood in this dump,' she says, taking our confirmation print-out. 'We even had a banner made up for you – I hope you don't mind?'

Over in the corner is a tacked-up sheet with "The Groveses Folk Rock Tonite" painted in what looks like fence stain. It's the sort of thing you see tied up on a flyover telling Auntie Val "Happy 50th Birthday" and hanging limp with last night's rain. Well, you have to give it to her for trying. It's the first time anyone's made an effort for us.

'Oh, cheers – that's the nuts!' Sandy says and immediately jumps into the preparations for our gig tonight. I let her get on with it. I'm whacked after driving, and the smell of hops and the heat from the fire are making me feel claustrophobic. I excuse myself and plonk my bum down in a booth. It's next to a bookcase which is handy because it looks like Sandy's going to natter with that barmaid for a long while. They're already cackling like a pair of witches.

I drum my fingers on the sticky table as I scan the stuff on the shelves. It's the usual crap that tourists leave behind – Caravan Club stuff, battered Ordnance Survey maps and some well-thumbed romances, the sort with the pages folded over at the dirty bits. I pick a grimy map and spread it out on the table. Some of these roads probably don't exist anymore.

Bugger that. I whip my phone out to write a cheeky status, but the *no Internet connection* notification of doom appears before I even think of one. There's not even any network coverage for a text. I shove the phone back in my pocket and have another look at the shelves.

Sandy's chuckle rings through the place as I pick up a crinkled women's magazine, thinking I could have a laugh at a true-life story. Then I decide there's only so many times you can read about a woman with one nipple too many and sling it back on the shelf.

That's when I see it and wonder why I hadn't before. A massive, leather-bound tome – because that's the only way to describe a book like that – complete with brass thingies, wedged between two shelves. I lean across the table and tug, but some idiot's got it well and truly stuck. It might come if I use two hands, so I hook my fingers either side and really go for it.

It finally gives, and my elbow flies back, hitting something hard. Whatever it is, falls and smashes.

'Well done, numb-nuts!'

I spin around and see Sandy looking at the glass of coke that I knocked out of her hand, now in bits on the flagstone floor. She thumps my shoulder with her empty hand.

'What d'you want to do that for?'

'It's all right, love! No harm done!' The barmaid's tottering over with another drink and a dustpan and brush, a wad of blue roll tucked in her armpit. 'I'll clear this – you just get started on those drinks.'

'Thanks, Karen,' Sandy says, as she slides in opposite me.

'Best mates already?' I smirk.

'Look - she's paying us for tonight *and* giving us free board, and you've just wrecked her floor. Just shut your mouth and be thankful.'

I want to laugh as she says it all in one breath before taking a mannish swig of her drink. That's typical Sandy – meaning well, in her own roundabout way. She smacks her lips and nods towards me.

'So, what have you got there, then?'

It takes me a while to figure out she means the book I've still got in my hands, and I drop it like a hot sausage. It thumps on the table, cover side down.

'Oh, right – I thought you and her were in it for the duration. Talking.'

Karen mumbles something about the cat's mother from near my knees as Sandy reaches over and slides the book towards her.

'This thing weighs a ton.' She bounces it up and down in her hands. I can see some of the cover between her fingers. Embossed in the leather is a mess of leaves, acorns and vines. It's got eyes, and it's freaking me right out, like it's staring me out.

I'm glad when red talons appear at the side of the table like

11

a grappling hook, distracting me. Karen hoists herself up from the floor, dustpan poised like a weapon. *The She-Warrior of Usher's Well.* I have to bite the inside of my cheek to keep from bursting, but Sandy has twigged it as well and pulls her hair in front of her mouth, trying to keep it together as our eyes meet, laughing.

'Done!' Karen beams with that weird self-satisfaction of people over a certain age, and her earrings jangle as she dusts her knees. I expect her to click-clack back to the bar when she leans over Sandy.

'Oh!' She crows. 'I knew it wouldn't take you long to find that old thing. Be right up your street, no doubt.'

Sandy heaves the book over and examines the leafy design on the front. She brushes her fingers over the top and bites her lip like she always does when she's excited about something.

'It's a Green Man,' she breathes. I haven't heard her breathe like that since we discovered foreplay, and I'm actually jealous of the bloody thing. She opens the book up and sniffs the paper. *Weirdo.*

'*Folk Songs Of Olde England*,' she reads. She starts turning the pages carefully. They look a bit crumbly and she's only a pair of gloves short of looking like an archivist.

'There's a lot in here I recognise,' says Sandy. *Oh, joy.* I'm not going to get any conversation out of her for the next few hours. *Thank you so much, Karen. That's right, bugger off back behind the bar. And thanks, me, for getting the bloody thing off the shelf in the first place.*

'Here's *Allison Gross*! And *Bold William Taylor*... oh, and this one looks really cool!'

'Isn't there a contents page or something?' I ask, desperate. *On second thoughts, don't tell me.* I don't fancy another lecture. I slump back in my seat and look around me as Sandy reels off more song titles and exclamations. There's a fruitie in the corner, and I doubt Karen reckons I'm underage seeing as we drove here. I might have a go on it in a minute. I'll try to win some petrol money.

I look to the bar to check if Karen's looking, just in case, but she's chatting to some old bloke with his arm on the bar top. When did he get here? I don't really like the look of him, he's perched on a stool and facing this way. He's listening to Karen but staring straight at me from under his flat cap, tumbler in hand. It's creeping me right out and I'm grateful when Sandy catches my eye.

'Look, I know this isn't your idea of fun,' she begins, shutting her eyes like she's steeling herself for something. *Captain Obvious strikes again.* If I weren't feeling uneasy, I'd make some smarmy comment like that. But we're here for her, and I want to make it nice for her. No rows like we've been having more and more of lately.

'Go on, then.' I reach over and tap the pages. 'See if I'm in there.'

It's done it. Her eyes spark right up.

'Righto!' She flicks through the pages. I didn't ask to be called Matty. It's a stupid name really, something you'd call a dog. But even though I'm not folk music's biggest fan, it's still pretty cool to share a name with a song and a bloody, gruesome one at that. And the Matty in the song bedded a rich older woman. That can't be bad.

The bloke at the bar's still staring at me. It might just be his way. When you hit a certain age, I think you lose any sense of politeness. There's just something about his eyes. It's not a blank stare like when you're looking at someone on the train but thinking of what's for tea. It's almost like he's studying me, and I wish he'd just piss off.

'You're psychic,' Sandy beams.

'Do what?'

'*Matty Groves*. It's in here. Whoring yourself out to old books, eh?' She peers at the words a while longer. 'Though I have to say I don't remember it ending like that.'

'Like what?' I forget about the creep at the bar. She's got my interest now. I've been forced to listen to different versions of the thing for the past few years, as well as play it in our sets. It must be different if Lady Folkly has twigged it. I swap sides and slide in next to her.

Sure enough, she's right. A solitary page is loose, but it doesn't look like it was ever attached because the paper's different, and the words are handwritten. There's one more verse starting from where the original ballad left off, when Lord Donald goes apeshit and kills Matty for shagging his wife, and then the wife for putting it about. This new verse is borderline spooky:

"A grave, a grave, she was put in, but now to take her out,
Lord Donald's wife of noble kin shall rise to walk about
As the mists do kiss the cliffs so white, and so the sea the sand,
I call on them to do their work; Lady Donald shall live again."

We read in silence, just taking it in.

'Poor show, mind. It doesn't even rhyme!' I nudge Sandy

and we crack up. Then something grips my shoulder, cold and hard as a vice, and I nearly choke.

'Bloody hell!'

'Matty, pack it up!' Sandy elbows me in the ribs, then her voice goes funny and almost posh like when she's talking to her supervisor at college. 'Sorry, sir. You gave him a bit of a fright.'

Sir? I look up into nose hair and, above that, the creepy eyes of the weirdo from the bar. He looks at me thoughtfully, moustache wiggling as he chews his lips.

'No trouble, love,' he says, finally. 'Young man.' He nods at me, then sits down opposite us. *Rude.*

'So, you're the Groveses, then.' He stares at us like he's weighing us up, then wets his lips like a real old codger. 'I must say I'm looking forward to the show tonight. It should be an interesting evening.'

Before I can ask him to leave or stop talking, Sandy speaks for the pair of us.

'Thanks very much, it means a lot.'

'And I see you found *that.*'

This is meant for me, as he catches my eye and nods at the book. It's feeling a bit too *Wicker Man* for me to answer.

'You'll have noticed the centre pages, no doubt.'

Are you kidding me? This bloke's really not doing himself any favours.

'Yes…' Sandy begins, cautiously. She looks at me, and I think we're on the same level. *What is his game and why won't he just get lost and, Christ, why hasn't he heard of mouthwash?* As if answering me, he knocks back his whiskey.

'You would do well not to read from that extra page. The

handwritten one. Don't even whisper the words if you can help it.'

'Leave them alone, you old git! Filling their heads with all that curse rubbish!' Karen's waving at us from behind the bar, and I could kiss her. *Thank you, glorious she-warrior.* 'Don't you take any notice of Laurence, my loves. It's his age, he gets a bit confused.'

'It is not rubbish, Karen!' Laurence slams a papery hand on the table and we all pop up like possessed Pringles lids. He sneers at us, and stands, shuffling towards the door. Karen shakes her head and waves a hand like she's telling us to forget it. Once the old boy's out of earshot, Sandy shakes my arm.

'Did you hear that?' Her eyes are wide. 'A *curse?*'

I nod, and then grin at her.

'A cursed book, eh? What a load of old bollocks!'

'Matty, don't.' She makes to put the book back on the shelf but I grab it off her.

'Matty, give it to me.'

'Don't tell me you believe that crap?'

'Please.' Her eyes are sparkling, and not in the good way. It's the usual prelude to me getting labelled a nasty prick or worse. She's filling up like she's about to let the floodgates open, and it makes my stomach twist up. It always does when I feel guilty for doing something. I don't want to spoil the first leg of the tour, but she has to learn.

She tries to snatch the book out of my hands. We struggle briefly, but I'm too strong for her and as she slips I end up smacking myself in the face with it.

'You stupid cow. What's up with you?'

She doesn't look at me but stands and pushes past me with her hands in her pockets.

'I'll get the instruments in. Don't even speak to me.'

Well done, you nasty prick.

***

It doesn't matter how many times I perform, I still get the nerves. I've been in the shitter twice already and my t-shirt has begun to stick to my back and we're only tuning up. Everyone in the village has turned out to watch us, or at least it feels that way. Sandy's fighting with the mic stand and I realise that we've brought the one that sticks, not the new one her dad bought for us, and I wonder if this is a sign that it's all going to go to pot because that would be just our luck. Today certainly seems to have started off that way.

Thankfully, she wrestles it into place and picks up her fiddle. She doesn't look at me as she sticks a finger from her free hand in her ear, ready for the accapella introduction we've practiced all week. Apparently it helps you keep in tune, but I think that's a load of bull and she does it to look old-school.

'Come you young men, come along,
With your music and your song!
Bring your lasses by the hand
For it's that love does command!'

I join in on the harmony, hands shaking on my guitar, but she catches my eye and finally smiles.

'Then to the maypole haste away,
For 'tis now our holiday!'

FOLKED UP

All eyes are on us as we bounce straight into a jig with its funny time signature. It's all right for her playing actual melodies but when you're just doing chords, it can be awkward. Christ, I wish we were playing rock. Maybe I'll ask if we can finally branch out, when things between us are sound again. Right now, we just have to get through this set.

We play a few of the old staples which appear to go down well with the locals. They're all near to death that it's hardly surprising. They go for any old bollocks as long as they've got a drink in their hand. My Nan was the prime example at the Christmas talent show. I've even twigged old Laurence tapping his foot in time near the bar. After a while, even I get into it. It's always the way, I can't help but get caught up in the energy – and even though I'd rather be playing rock, it's great to have people just listening to *us*.

We've just finished some tune about a sailor – I never take a lot of notice of the titles – and they all clap. Even Karen, who is still behind the bar, is pumping her fist and making "ooh-ooh!" noises like she's egging on a fight. It's funny to hear in the sleepy candlelight.

'Thanks very much, ladies and gentlemen,' Sandy says, running a hand through her sweat-stuck fringe. 'It's been brilliant having you all tonight. We'd like to say goodnight with murder most foul, as you do. This is a ballad called *Matty Groves,* but perhaps not as you know it.'

I assume she means because not everyone sings these songs the same way, but there's something about the way she's tensed up that makes me wonder. She looks at me and gives me one of her winks she thinks looks badass when she's beat me at a game. Something's up, but I can't ask what because we've started playing.

I keep my guard up throughout the song. I can't help but feel like Laurence is watching me. It's bollocks, of course, because everyone in this place is watching us, but there's something about the way his eyes dart between me and Sandy that makes me worry, like he's expecting us to slip up, or worse. He starts chewing on a finger and I have to look away, concentrating on another weird-arse time signature.

Sandy's just sung the last line, when Donald's killed the wife and asked her to be buried on top of the lover which always weirds me out a bit. We usually play a few more bars of music and end it there, but two bars in Sandy catches my eye, and mouths something at me. It looks like "carry on". She fishes something out of her pocket with her free hand, nodding her head as I continue strumming. It's just the sound of my guitar now and I wish she'd hurry with whatever she's got planned because I don't like feeling exposed like this.

She holds whatever it is up in front of her, but I don't even need to see what it is before she starts singing again. I flush with excitement for her. *Go on, girl.*

'*A grave, a grave, she was put in –*' she starts. That's done it. It's chaos near the bar as Laurence has his stool over and starts pushing his way towards us.

'Stop! You don't know what you're doing!' he cries as he stumbles past other punters who are getting arsey with him. Sandy's still singing but gives me a funny old look when she twigs Karen, who's jumped out from behind the bar and is trying to pull him back.

'Sit down, you old prat!' she whines. 'You're spoiling it!'

He shrugs her off with the strength of someone half his age.

'For goodness' sake, listen!'

Nobody does.

'*–Lady Donald shall live again*,' Sandy finishes. Everything's tense as I do a final few strums, but nothing happens. Laurence stands, hunched and puffing, and everyone turns to look at the div who nearly ruined the set. Karen gives him a shove and starts to take him back to his place.

I don't see what happens next. I only hear the scream.

2

Matty

It's got to be Sandy pulling my leg – screaming like something's up and trying to make me feel like I'm in the wrong. I don't get a chance to find out. The whole place erupts in noise, screams coming from all sides in full-on surround sound.

But why the hell is everyone running away, scraping chairs and dropping glasses, all trying to get out the door as quickly as they can? I turn to look at Sand, but I'm garroted by my guitar strap. The instrument's torn from my body, the strap breaking. It flies across the makeshift stage, just missing Sand's head by centimetres and smashing up against the wall. She doesn't flinch – not at the near miss, not at her own fiddle beating itself against the floor. Not even at the banner flapping madly in an invisible gale-force wind. Instead, her eyes are popping out of her head as she stares at the page from the book. She drops it and it's like its mass changes mid-fall. It stiffens and slams itself against the floor and it's now that I realise it's glowing white, lighting up the joint like Blackpool illuminations, shooting off sparks, and shaking violently. The flagstones under my feet grumble in what feels like an epic earthquake, but it's all coming from that page. What the actual —?

Sandy's gone at it with her mic stand, swinging it axe-style. It bangs and bangs into the ground, but it's doing nothing but sending even more sparks everywhere. Got it – *destroy the page, curb the magical bollocks*. If that's even what this is.

I crouch down, struggling to balance, and stick a hand out to grab it.

'Shit!'

I fly back and land on my arse. My hand's burning hot and tingling all at once, and it's bloody sore. Did the bastard just *electrocute* me?

'Matty!'

Sandy rushes for me. It all happens too quickly. The ground's still shaking and she's coming towards me, but the page is there, between us, flashing whiter than white. A slit of white shoots up, slicing my view of Sand in two. No, it's a *hole*, and it looks like invisible hands are fighting to open it up wider as the sides tremble and slowly part.

I can see her through the white flashes, it's like looking through net curtains. Her hand passes through it, grabbing mine. She grasps so tightly that my arm jolts as something tries to snatch her away. Our fingers separate as her legs are yanked backwards. She chins the floor as she falls. I hear her swearing and shouting as she's dragged backwards into the white making me go cold. They're distant, and it's not possible to sound distant when she's so *close*. I try to grab onto her hands, like claws as they flail, trying to catch hold of something, anything.

I'm too slow. My guts do a somersault when I can't see her anymore. She's not there. She's not anywhere. It's starting to close up, slowly but surely, and my heart boxes my ears as I scramble to my feet and take a few steps back. Then I start for a running jump.

'Don't!'

Jangling hands yank my shoulders back and nearly have me over. It's Karen, and she looks like she's about to cry, her face pale and crumpled. Everyone else is gone. All except her, and someone else.

'I warned you! Didn't I warn you?' Laurence is edging towards us, his leathery hand shielding his squinting eyes.

He did warn us. We didn't listen, but then why should we have done? Who would listen to this absolute bollocks that you couldn't make up even if you tried? I don't need to be treated like some kid who's misbehaved. I don't have time for it.

'What the hell *is* this? Where's she gone?'

'A place that far predates our own.'

What does that even mean? He clamps a hand on my arm but I shrug him off.

'Back off, you old bastard,' I spit at him. 'I've got to go after her.'

'But –'

'I'm *going* – end of.' Because if I don't go now, the hole will close and I don't know where Sandy is or what's happened.

He seems to deflate but there's something in his watery old eyes that looks nostalgic, like he'd have done the same fifty years ago. Maybe he did, maybe the old prat's a glutton for punishment. He looks at Karen, whose whole being seems to be saying "no, don't go, Matty, because I want to call it a night and have a cup of tea and I can't ruddy well do that if you go off because there'll be lengthy legal implications". He looks at all that, then back at me and nods.

'Then you must hurry. Trust nobody but believe. You have to believe!'

I don't believe in an awful lot but I believe in what I see and I don't even yell a goodbye as I launch myself into the absolute load-of-bollocks, white-net-curtain, electric hole of doom.

3
Sandy

'She will need to die, sire.'

They're the words I hear, over and over, echoing like I'm underground. I think I heard them in my dream. I don't remember what happened, but there was talk of magic, and murder. I'm awake, but sort of half-dreaming still. My head's banging and I'm frightened to open my eyes. It's in case I do it too quickly, and they go into that awful, tight kind of spasm that hurts like a bitch and makes your eyes water for the first ten minutes of the day. I try to move my hand to give them a massage before I open them, but I can't lift it. It's pinned down by something. Something heavy, warm, and hairy.

I chance it and snap my eyes open. To the left of me is a massive, nay gargantuan dog, who sighs in his sleep through his nose – I'm guessing it's a he, purely because of his size. The smell of his breath is a meaty, bad-teethy concoction that makes me want to chuck. He's as grey as a rain cloud, and shaggy like Teddy Warbucks who still comes to bed with me sometimes. I think he's a deerhound – like a greyhound, but fuzzier and way bigger. His head has got to be the size of a small kid, taking up the whole pillow on his side. *Meathead,* I think, and laugh – quietly, so as not to have him wake up and rip my throat out. Maybe I'll greet him when he's awake, as long as his temperament's all right.

I shut my eyes again, still heavy with sleep. Where did the meathead come from? And what's happened, exactly? I go through what I can remember in my head. We were performing – that's right; we were touring. I didn't pass out, did I? I hope not, I can't stand people fussing over me. Did we go straight to bed, in our room at the inn? No, there were no animals allowed, else we'd have brought Ozzy, mum's Jack Russell, with us. Then, where –?

I sit up sharply, tearing my hand out from under the dog, and my head rushes painfully. There was a curse. There was that book. All that mad business back at the inn, like poltergeist goings-on. I go cold as I look about me. The dog doesn't move, but there's definitely movement in the room. It's dark, but I can just make out curtains swaying gently at the end of the room. There's sunlight eking through underneath.

Sunlight. Christ, is it morning? Have I slept right through? I rush over and try to draw the curtains open. The heaviest curtains in existence. I heave and finally feel the sun's warmth on my face. It's fresh, like the windows are open. There aren't any windows. Through the curtains I'm let out onto a square stone balcony, with a low balustrade decorated with arches. Beyond that, there's green.

I step gingerly out and look all around me. This is definitely still the countryside, nothing but fields as far as the eye can see. That familiar smell clings to my nostril; dung and rapeseed. I inhale as deeply as I can, hoping it'll clear my head.

I turn back to the room. The bed I've just got off is a massive four-poster affair, with crimson sheets and a thick eiderdown, the same colour purple as my favourite chocolate. The dog's rucked it all up around him since I left, and I wonder if he's gotten cold without me.

There are candles burning on a heavy oak sideboard, and tapestries with hunting scenes covering the stone walls. These have to be worth some money. I can see they're old, but they're in far better condition than anything I've seen on the antiques programmes on telly. They might have been bought yesterday.

The entire place looks like one of the medieval mock-ups in the castles that Matty and I visit a lot, only far better quality.

'Matty.' The word comes out automatically, and the dog lifts his head to stare at me. I think it's trying to decide whether or not I'm talking to him. Then he rolls over onto his front and has a bit of a stretch before plopping down off the bed. I don't feel scared as he trots over to me and rubs his great big fuzzy head into my belly. I take this as the okay to fuss him and scratch behind his ears, and his eyes close gently as he makes soft licking noises and leans all his weight into me.

'You going to help me find out what's up, then?' I ask him, though I think it's more to myself, trying to break the silence. But when I start towards the door, he keeps by my side. There's no door to this room, only an archway next to the sideboard. So, feeling a bit like an adventurous tomboy from the books I read when I was little, I hook a hand on the stone and poke my head around the corner.

4

Matty

I'd run into that hole, sprinting at full speed, expecting my feet to connect with the ground on the other side. I didn't expect to fall, but I do. My guts are in my throat, like they were on the free-fall ride Sand dragged me on last summer, and my head's spinning to the point I think I'm going to chuck.

It's cold, but then you try falling fast into the void. Only it's not a void. The whole electric net curtain effect fades into mist as I tumble, and the ground's coming in fast. There are trees. Lots of them. They look like trees that'll hurt.

There's barely time to shut my eyes. There's clawing at my arms and things digging in and scratching as I plunge straight through branches. I do a full-on belly flop onto an especially meaty limb and stop. It's caning like one of the hench gym squad has socked me one after college, but to be honest I really couldn't give a shit. I'm intact. *Alive.*

I just lie there for a bit in the tree, catching my breath and sweating, before I take a look down. It's not too far from the ground, so I shift into a sitting position and jump down. The fall's taken more out of me than I thought because my legs buckle as I land, and I go arse over tit. But it's all right, because there's nobody around to call me a prat.

Looking around, it's green. Very green. *Too* green. I've never seen so many shades of it in my life and reckon I must be in a forest. Well, that'd explain the trees, anyway. There's no sign that anyone's been here, but then wild flora tends to have that sort of feel. There's no sign of where I should go, no sign of Sandy. No sign of where I am, even. For the first time, I'm actually lost. *Proper* lost.

Then I remember something, and get to my feet, feeling a bit smug about it, actually. This must be how a boffin feels when they're the only one who knows the answer out of their entire class. There's some book I read when I was little, and I remember that moss will always grow on the north-facing side of trees. Or something. *Get in.* I touch the trunk of the nearest tree, and then I twig that it's only useful if I know which direction I need to go in, and I most definitely don't. *Bugger.*

'Sandy!' I start shouting for her. Maybe I'm hoping she'll jump up from behind a bush like it's a game and she'll shriek through tears that I should see the look on my face. Or she might be hiding in a hollow tree or something, but all these ones around me look very solid. I kick the dirt at one knobbly base and plonk my arse down on a fat, upraised root. It's sharper than I'm expecting and the pain shoots through my arse-bone, if that's even a thing.

Oh, you dozy prat. You can ring *her.* She always takes her mobile with her, even if she does think technology's going to kill the human race. Still, I reckon if she's lost, she'd rather use that monstrosity than hunt down a phone box for the sake of being retro. I root around in both pockets, then jump up to check my back pocket by my sore arse. There's only a few balls of tissue and a sweet wrapper covered in lint. It must have come out of my pocket when I fell, and that's just bloody typical when I'm due an upgrade.

It's a good few minutes of feeling sorry for myself, trying to think of what to do next, before I feel something digging on my shoulder. I turn my head and leap out of my bloody skin. A black, beady eye looks at me, unblinking and unnerving. It's a crow, and it shifts itself from foot to foot as though it's about to make itself comfortable, or shit down my back.

'Oh no you don't. Find yourself another perch.' I try to glare at it, but there's no real way of glaring at birds unless you're in the queue for fried chicken. 'I've got enough on my plate already.'

Nothing. I try to shrug it off, and then brush it off, but it grinds its feet in with what I suspect is indignation. *Impossible.* You get those birds that look a bit up themselves, like peacocks or pheasants, but I'm fairly certain that birds do not express emotion in their feathery faces. I scowl and cross my arms as I look at him – and I'm pretty sure it's a him, just because of the attitude – but talk away at him because it's nice to have a bit of company.

'You don't care that I'm a prick, do you? None of this would've happened if I'd only *listened*. And now Sandy's gone, and I don't know what to do, and you're taking the rise.' I look at him again. Something's not right. It's the eyes again.

'Did you just wink at me?' It's a rhetorical thing, but then the little bugger nods at me. Not just a birdy twitch, this is a proper nod, and a slow one like the cheeky sod thinks I'm an idiot.

'*Shit*. You can understand me.' I can't help myself and start laughing, scratching the corner of my mouth like I do when I'm embarrassed. I'm not embarrassed now, but the crow's still staring at me, like it's waiting for me to say something else. And I'm fully aware that I'm talking to a bird like a loony, and I probably am a loony, but Laurence told me to believe, didn't he? It's absolutely mental, but I venture:

'Can you take me to Sandy?'

There's a great big flap of feathers as he flies off to the right of me, light flashing off his wings as he speeds through the trees. I'm not half glad I'm wearing my trainers as I go after him.

5
Sandy

The room leads out into a long passageway – all stone, no carpets. Looking to the left there's a bit of a dead end, with just another glass-less window. We head right, and start walking, passing more tapestries, metal sconces with no torches in them, and heavy bits of wood furniture. I'm grateful for the tick-tack of the dog's nails on the stone next to me, because I don't think I like this place. I roll the sleeves of my hoodie down as it's nippy along here and pick up the pace.

'Wither do you go, child?'

Wither? Bloody child? I spin around, the soles of my skate shoes squeaking on the stone. Some man with a milky eye and an epic beard-and-hair combo is looking me up and down, arms folded like Mum when I get back late from rehearsals. He's wearing a long tunic that makes him look like some druid out of his nut. But where'd he spring from? There were no other rooms down that end of the corridor. I wonder if he's been in my room all that time and I just hadn't seen him, and that's a really creepy thought.

I can't let it show that I'm worried, so I spread my feet apart and put my hands on my hips. I've seen the chavvy girls do it at the bus stop when they're about to accuse their significant others of putting it about because Becca saw him snogging Tanya behind the science labs, and it always makes them ooze "hard".

'D'you mean where?'

Milky winces, trying to understand.

'Prithee…?'

'Where was I going – that's what you asked me, isn't it?'

He smiles slightly. The dog makes a sneezing sound before standing in front of me. Milky takes a step towards us, then thinks better of it as the dog's hackles go up and he snarls. Crap, is he *protecting* me?

'Quite. After all the trouble his lordship has taken to make you comfortable, you would take your leave of us?'

His language seems too obvious to be real. Theatrical, almost. And then I look at that blind eye of his and twig how easy it is to get contact lenses, and I think I get what this is all about and start laughing.

'I see. Yep – very funny, Matty. All this effort to prove a point, you sad bastard.' I shake my head and thrust my hands in my pockets. 'Well, you really had me going for a bit then. You can come out now, you utter knob.'

Milky, or rather Laurence playing Milky, cocks his head to one side like he's still trying to understand. He's not half playing it well.

'You came alone, Sandy.' He waves his hand like a villain in a superhero film, and the sconces on the wall burst into flame, illuminating the passage. I don't jump, but the dog does and heads somewhere behind my legs. I'd like to thump Milky for scaring him, but I'm also genuinely impressed. It all looks so bloody real.

'Here, how'd you manage that?' I say, looking all about me for a light switch, or wires, or any proof that it's a trick.

Milky crosses his arms and tuts, which really puts my back up.

'A magician reveals his secrets not – is that not so?'

'Well, you can whip that stupid fake beard off, at least,' I spit, because enough is enough. 'Where's Matty?'

His face twists up in a way that I don't quite get. It's either amusement or proper worry. Or both.

'Who is this… Matty?'

'Come off it. Matty, the numb-nuts. My *boyfriend?*' I don't add the "duh".

'Ah.'

'Problem?'

'This was not meant to happen. There wasn't to be a boy.'

'Oh, give it a rest, will you?' I shout. 'How about packing up your tricks and getting us back to the pub?'

His mouth's smiling, but the eyes are putting me off. I take a step back and feel my legs up against the dog who's as stiff as a board. I get it, I'm not meant to trust this guy. He's most definitely not Laurence, I can see that now. This bloke's even older, even more wrinkled. Even more cold.

'But you are back, my dear. His lordship will be ecstatic to see you finally up and about. He's something very particular planned for you.'

Like fun has this "lordship" got something planned for me.

I don't even say anything to the creep. I just storm off down the corridor, the dog alongside me, and I don't even look back to see if Milky is following. I've got to get away, and fast.

6
Matty

After following the crow and doing my quota of cardio for the week, the trees disappeared bit by bit and gave way to a clearing with a bit of a hill. I thought the bird might have stopped there, but it flew straight on and took a sky dive over the crest. When I reach the top, I see a solitary tower in the distance. An actual stone tower, a higgledy-piggledy thing that some tart would live in in a fairy-tale, plonked in the middle of a field like it's been dropped out of the sky. And the crow's just flown straight into the window at the very top.

I circle and circle the place for ages, but there's no way I'm getting in. There's no door, and absolutely no way I'm climbing the bastard. I've got to rest and work out my options like a sensible person would. That's what Sand would tell me to do. What am I going to do without her, when she's the one that keeps me straight, out of trouble? I've *got* to find her.

No use moaning, mind. Christ, I want a fag, but my ciggies are long gone. I chew the callous on my index finger and lean against the wall of the tower, thinking about possible ways in. The stone's lovely and soft on my back. And squidgy. And squirmy.

What the actual –? I jump up and spin around to have a butcher's, to make sure I'm not imagining things. The stones are *moving*, twisting out of place and opening up a person-sized arch. There are steps inside, twisting up into darkness. I poke my head in and decide that English Heritage obviously haven't got around to sorting this place yet. It doesn't look like it's been touched in centuries, and it stinks. It smells like damp houses on steroids, like the ones next to the chippy back home.

'Crow?' The bird better not get offended by the rubbish name I've given him. Do birds even take offence? I wait for as long as I think is polite before stepping in and calling again. There's still no answer. I hear subtle grinding behind me, but before I twig what it means or how to stop it, the stones move back into place. It's dark, it stinks, and I'm trapped. *Bollocks.*

I swallow hard. There's no two ways about it – I need to go up. There's just enough light coming from the mossy cracks and holes in the wall that I can make out where to put my feet. The stone's dipped through what looks like centuries of people treading up and down and worn smooth. I stick a hand on each wall, where any sane person would have put a banister – you know, just for shits and safety – to steady myself as I go.

'Bastard!' I walk through something that feels like a web and I go all cold because I don't do spiders. I'm done with all this now. My legs are hurting where these steps are so steep and dodgy, I'm tired and I've had enough. So, I stop and cup my hands around my sweaty gob.

'Anyone up there?'

I don't think I'm expecting an answer. I just about shit

myself when a voice calls down to me.

'Do come up, little Matty Groves! We have not all day!'

Nope. I'm done. They know my name. They know I'm *here*. I do a one-eighty and start marching straight back down until I remember that I'm holed up.

I wonder if Sandy's scared, like I am now. If she's thinking about me like I am her. She's hard, she can take care of herself way better than I can.

Doesn't matter. I've got no choice.

I try to gather all the balls I've got within me, take a breath, and shift up the rest of the steps two at a time.

I'm sweating when I get to the top. I'm in a room of some sort. It's pitch black apart from a sliver of white-grey sky from the solitary arched window. It's the same one the crow flew up to. He's not there now.

'Hello?' I puff.

Something behind me slams and all the hairs on me stand to attention as I twig a distinct noise. That's the noise of a locking door, like you get in horror films. There was definitely nobody behind me on the stairs. *Don't be so bloody ridiculous – man up.* I step forward onto something that rolls slightly and then cracks under my foot. It feels like a pencil but sounds suspiciously like bone.

'Please.' I feel like a massive wally, talking to myself, but it makes me feel just that little bit better. 'I don't like this.'

'You do not like my home?'

Shit! That was right in my ear. I stumble backwards. My legs bang into something heavy. Whatever it is chucks red light out suddenly, like it's just been switched on. The light swings about all over the place, like the lights at a really naff wedding disco. I think I see the shadow of something heading towards me in the illuminations. It's tall, and horribly ghost-shaped, but I'm sure it's a woman given the voice.

'It was redone only weeks ago. Still, 'tis irrelevant. I have been expecting you, sir.'

I grab onto the heavy thing behind me, cold and solid, and steady myself on my hurting, trembling legs.

'What d'you mean, you've been expecting me? Here, and how did you know my name?' It sounds more like a squeak than a demand, and my throat feels like a sponge covered in grease like when you wash up after a fry-up.

'*Oh!*' The woman's voice buzzes through my bones. 'Forgive me, I do not entertain often. *Bescín!*'

There's a click of fingers inches from my face and immediately the room's lit up like somebody's put the big light on. I sort of wish they hadn't.

'Better.'

The lying bloody cow. There's too much to take in, and none of it is good. Bookcase, full of tomes. Cluster of brooms. Jars lined up on a rickety shelf. Tapestries and charts. The crow, staring at me from on top of what looks like a skull. And a quick glance down tells me I'm holding onto a massive pot. A *cauldron.* I'd piss myself laughing if it wasn't real, but it is. It's happening, and an invisible vice squeezes my chest as I put two and two together.

I point a finger at her, trying to assert my authority. I'm asserting nothing because my finger is shaking like a geriatric, but at least it starts my voice up again.

'You're a bloody *witch*.'

She looks down at her cloak, which is miles too big for her, like she's discovering herself for the first time – hands on her chest, face covered by wild black hair streaked with grey.

'Well done, sir!' She laughs, meeting my eyes. Hers are green. She might have been a looker were she twenty years younger. And not magic – I don't particularly want to hang about to find out whether it's the good or bad stuff she deals in, either.

I swallow hard and begin to edge around the cauldron. Whatever she is, I have to get away from her.

'This is mental. Witches aren't–'

'Real? I assure you, we are.'

As though to prove a point, she swoops down and grabs a stick – tell a lie, *wand* – from off the floor, near my feet. That must have been what I stepped on, though I wouldn't dare tell her. She touches the tip with her tongue, and it immediately glows that same red colour as whatever was in the cauldron. Then she points the bastard thing at me, and I do the only thing that comes into my worthless-but-still-wanting-to-be-alive head. *Grovel.*

'Please don't hurt me!'

'Idiot boy – wherefore should I wish to damage you? Such a... *handsome* young man I never did see in my life.'

My eyes are welded shut, but now they explode open with wanting to laugh.

'You bloody *what*?'

'I knew you would be. I have a knack for these things,' she breathes, running that wand all the way down my front like a scalpel. 'And now, little Matty Groves, you can stay here with me forever.'

I can't work out what her deal is, but it's a whole other kind of nervous sweat I'm soaked in now. I begin to feel my way around the cauldron with my hands, not taking my eyes off her and that wand. *One step at a time, mate. And don't annoy her, else it's kiss-your-arse-goodbye time.*

I swallow hard.

'Look, er, madam–'

She smiles even wider at that.

'*Allison*, please.'

'Allison, then,' I say. It's weird, the word feels right in my mouth, like it's familiar. Like I know her. Like it *fits* her. All at once I feel calmer, but then I remember the million different things my stupid mouth could say, and the consequences they'd bring. 'Look, it's a nice offer, but...'

I can see the panic in her face now. It's some ghost of a fear of rejection, and my guts twist up. Shit, I'm not feeling sorry for her, am I? The bitch could kill me.

We've made a full circle of the cauldron. She grabs onto the lip and squeezes as she leans forward and stares at me, with wide, brimming, unblinking eyes.

'Is it a mantle of red scarlet? A shirt of the softest silk? Or perhaps it is gold – anything you desire shall be thine if you will only stay and be a friend to me!'

She goes to grab my shirt, but I step back just in time. Her face crumples, and she sinks, doubled over like she's had a dodgy curry and a few pints.

No way. This doesn't feel right, this isn't what witches are meant to do. They're nasty, sometimes sexy, magical women that'd curse you as soon as look at you. They don't beg to be mates with you. It's pathetic. But there's something about the things she's offered me that sets off alarm bells somewhere in my head. Like the name felt right for her, I swear somebody's tried to give away that stuff before. But I can't think of that now, I need to get my head back in the game and do what I came here to do.

'I desire – oh, I *want* to find Sandy! I want my girlfriend back, that's what I want!'

Allison's head snaps up, like a marionette, eyes still wide. Without blinking, she pushes herself upright and nods.

'Very well,' she says, finally shutting her eyes and setting her jaw. It's that same face anyone pulls when they're trying to digest bad news or calm themselves down. I've got a feeling she's doing both. 'Then if you cannot stay, I shall have to *make* you stay.'

Oh, good.

7

Sandy

It was no good. This whole building's like a maze, one epic, almost-Medieval maze and Milky caught up with me in the end, with two big burly blokes in tow who I wasn't going to take my chances with. So now I've got to see this lord. It's all very ceremonial, considering I'm technically only chilling in the bloke's house. Still, Milky – whose actual name is Thackeray, which I keep shortening it to "Thacks" in my head because you have to do these things – tried ordering me to change my clothes earlier on. It seems hoodie and jeans don't quite meet the standards for "ladies", but I couldn't give a toss. The dog backed me up on this one, growling at Thacks when he raised his voice to me. I reckon we will be friends.

The dog is with me now, nuzzling his lovely head into my lap while I sit to attention in this hall. The wood of the chair's hurting my bum a bit and I'm sweating my eyeballs out because not only am I starting to get a bit nervous about meeting this lord, but they've got a fire going in the stone hearth in the centre of the hall. It's bloody *May*. What are this lot on?

There's movement at the far end. The wooden doors open slightly, and Thacks slides in, robes all a-rustle. He looks really pleased with himself. Which is my cue to scowl.

'Lord Donald will join us presently,' he says, sitting himself down opposite me and helping himself to what I assume is his lordship's wine. I stare at the goblet he pours into – it looks like a pewter, and little designs are etched into the sides and up the stem. I can make out greyhounds, hares and trees all twinkling in the firelight. It's pretty, something I wouldn't mind having in my house when I finally move out and get my own place with Matty. The magic's gone when Thacks takes it away from his lips and thick wine, almost black, trickles down the side. It looks sticky, and an awful lot like blood.

Then something in my mind clicks – he just mentioned a Lord Donald. Like Lord Donald from *Matty Groves*, Child ballad 81, the one Matty and I cover. The one we were told not to sing, but we did anyway, then all that mental stuff happened in the pub. There's no way, is there? That there actually is a curse, and that I was right all along? Matty is not half going to cop an earful when I get my hands on him.

'What's the deal with all of this?' I shift in my seat and scratch behind the dog's ears. He makes me feel calm, even confident.

Thackeray stares at the goblet and rolls it back and forth with his thumb and fingers, rings clanging against the stem.

'Which deal? We struck one not.'

'No – deal's what you say when you mean issue. The meaning of something. Whatever you want to call it.' It's no good. He's giving me that pained look again, and it's driving me potty.

'Oh, just leave it, then!' I slam my fist into the table which makes the dog jump. 'What's the point talking to you if you don't understand me? Christ, even the dog's got more brains than you!'

'That mangy cur is one reason you are come to us, my dear.'

This voice isn't Thacks. This one is new, coming from the other end of the hall, and it's got more life in it than Thacks's. I turn to see if it's another weirdo.

Striding towards us is a thin bloke – or I'm assuming he's thin. Like Thacks, he's got massive robes twirling all about him making him look more sizable than I think he is, because his face is almost gaunt, finished with a greying goatee any nu-metal singer would kill for. He looks the part of a lord, and to be fair he's got some go in him for an almost-wrinkly. I can't get distracted though – I have Matty, and I need to get out of here, wherever that is.

I mustn't lose my nerve now, so I stroke the dog, for luck or something, and throw my head back in what I hope's a couldn't-care-less way.

'So, you're Lord Donald, then?'

He sits down further down the table.

'Quick girl. *Clever girl* – as planned.'

I sigh and stand up.

'Look, are you'se lot going to stop talking like you're in on a joke and tell me what's going on? Why am I here? Why am I "planned"?'

Thacks jumps out of his seat and reaches a hand across the table, squeezing my cheeks so hard that my teeth start digging in.

'You will hold your tongue, trollop!'

He's strong. I claw at his bony fingers that are around my chops, but they won't budge. The dog jumps up and latches onto Thacks's arm. He squawks and let's go of my face. He tries to shake him off, but the dog is stuck on tight, paws on the table and pulling as though he's tying to tear the arm out of its socket.

'I don't know what century you're living in, mate, but I'm not having that! "Trollop" my eye,' I huff. 'Down, meathead,' I tell the dog, my voice softer, and pull gently at his neck. He yawns, his mouth open, and Thacks draws his arm back quickly, muttering some rubbish about the dog I don't want to hear. I just glare.

Donald hasn't said a thing. He's just watching me with interest, chin resting on his hand. He scratches at his 'tache and nods at something behind me.

'You see yon portrait hanging, there?'

I turn in my seat. There's a painting on the wall, above the hearth where that ridiculous fire's going, that I haven't taken much notice of before. It's a portrait of a woman, dressed in green. Her hands are folded in her lap and her head is tilted to one side. Something about her expression makes me think she was trying not to laugh when she sat for it, and that makes me smile for the first time since I've been here. She's a beautiful woman, middle-aged, but her dark hair hangs loose around her face and bosom that suggests that she would've been young at heart. I'm staring at her, and then shake my head as I recognise the horror-film territory we're in danger of entering – backstory ahoy, I reckon, and it'd be laughable if I was watching this on a screen or reading it in a book. But I've got to ask Donald, so I can try to get answers.

'She's lovely. But what about her?'

Donald's biting at a thumbnail, staring at the portrait. He can't take his eyes off it, and it doesn't seem to have registered that I'm talking to him. Could it be that she's –?

'Lady Benevolence Donald,' Thacks tells me. Can this bloke read minds or what?

'Sorry, Benevolence? That can't be an actual name, can it?'

The dog gives a little cry in his throat and puts his head in my lap again. I take it that means it can.

Thacks sounds bored.

'You'll be aware of the ballad, of course. "A holiday, a holiday, the –"'

'"The first one of the year."' I nod. 'That's *Matty Groves*. We sing it.'

Donald carries on biting his fingers, but talks through them, cutting through whatever Thacks is about to come out with.

'Have you ever thought about folk songs and ballads? From whence they come?'

I play with the dog's ears.

'They're songs of the people, passed down. That's why they're *folk* songs.' I want to add "you div", but think I'd better hold it.

'Indeed. They tell of life, of reality. Of truth.'

I know what he's getting at. He *is* the Lord Donald in the song. And if the story's true, he killed his wife, the woman in the portrait, for having it away with Matty Groves. But it can't be my Matty. The song's centuries old. If I'm going to go along with all this, that I've been brought back in time, fine. I'll take that for the time being, mad as it is. But I still don't know what my part is in all this.

'There is no need for you to fret, Sandy,' Thacks says. 'After all, you did take the pains to make this possible. You spoke the words.'

Got it. The extra page from the book. What an idiot.

'So, you're bringing this Benevolence woman back from the dead, is that it?'

'Aye.'

I start to shake. I think I know where this is going. There's been some sort of a mix-up, they've got the wrong Matty and they're going to take it out on him by doing me in. Life for a life, or what have you.

Donald clears his throat and pours himself some wine.

'Our wedding is to take place three days from now–'

Hang about. Wedding?

'The anniversary of her passing. May Day.'

'Yeah, yeah, but what wedding?'

Thacks chuckles.

'Have you fox-grease, my lord? I do believe this one needs her ears unblocked!'

I'll box his ears in a minute if he keeps on. Then it dawns on me.

'No way. Look, I'm sorry for your loss and all, really, I am. But there's no way I'd ever marry an old perv like you.'

Donald cocks his head like a dog.

'Tell me, girl, what a "perv" may be?'

'You're really not doing yourself any favours, asking that.'

I can hear my heartbeat in my ears. There's no way I'll make it out of this room. I've been looking around, weighing up my options, and even if I do get out, I'm sure there'll be more staff in this place who'll catch me.

'It is you who'll not do yourself any favours in resisting, girl. Everything has been arranged.'

The dog nudges me in the back. I turn in my seat, ready to fuss him, and then I notice the iron companion set next to the fire. Pokers, shovels, and other long pointy bits are all lined up and gagging for me to grab one. You could do a fair bit of damage with one of them.

'And how's that going to help bring Benevolence back?'

I've got to stall, keep him talking, as I try to subtly make out I'm leaning back for the dog. I manage to unhook one of the smaller pokers, just small enough to hide up my sleeve. Even having it on me makes me feel happier.

Thacks speaks up.

'Once married, you will be Lady Donald. And when the blood of Lady Donald spills, so shall the other rise.'

'You're gonna *kill* me? You're up the wall, the pair of you!'

Quick as I can, I whip the poker from out of my sleeve and drive it into Thacks's hand. He cries out in a way that makes my belly flip and the dog whimper. It goes deeper than I thought it would, straight through, and gets stuck in the wood of the table, pinning the hand down. *Bugger.* I try to pull it out, but it only makes Thacks moan more and now Donald's coming towards me. I grab another whatsit from the iron set quick , ready to batter the bastard, but as I turn to face him, my chest goes tight. He's got my meathead by the scruff of his neck and is holding a knife to his throat.

'Any more tricks, girl, and Matty returns to his earth.'

I drop my would-be weapon.

' "Matty"? You're telling me the *dog* is –?'

Donald twists the scruff, making the dog whimper.

'Funny how truths become so easily distorted. The ballad would tell you I killed the brute who would besmirch my lady's honour. Nay, death would have been too noble for him. Thackeray's power is such that even peasants dare not believe it, so they merely altered the tale. Is that not the way of folksong?'

I look at Thacks. He doesn't look capable of anything at the minute, wincing as he tries to get the poker out, blood trickling between the knobbly parts of his hand. But didn't he say he was a magician? Didn't he light up the passageway, and more than likely magic me here with that book? Stands to some kind of reason he can turn adulterers into animals.

I swallow.

'Please don't hurt the dog. I'll do whatever you want.'

Thacks finally gets the poker out, and he clamps his good hand over the wound to try and stop the blood that's started to gush. It's already stained his sleeve.

'You would not believe this wench's lies, my lord?'

Donald lets go of Meathead – no, Matty – and sheaths the knife.

'Ladies lie not. Girls, on the other hand, must *learn.*'

8
Matty

I swallow and try to sound big.

'You can't *make* me stay.'

Allison raises her wand, rolling it between her fingers. The grain of the wood starts glowing like the end of a cigarette, only green this time.

'Yet I can make it your only option. I shall simply turn you into a *wyrm*.'

I'd react, either laughing or grovelling again, but now I know what's up. You just don't forget songs where the singer gets turned into a worm. Especially when it's your own bloody band that's playing it.

'You're *Allison Gross*!'

I grin when I realise I've got one up on her. She just stands there, mouth opening and closing like she's broken, as if I've shown her magic way stronger than her own.

'Prithee, *how* –?'

The wand's smoking. I don't think it's meant to be doing that. It's definitely not meant to be doing that, going by the look on her face as it lights right up. I shut my eyes, but the bang makes my ears ring. It shakes the room. Heat whooshes into my face and all around me. I can hear the crow squawking in the corner somewhere and I sort of hope he's not become fried chicken.

I expect to open my eyes and see everything from ground level, worm or otherwise. But when I do, I'm still holding onto the cauldron. I'm still me-height. Allison, though, is gone. Her cloak and wand are in a heap on the floor, smouldering away.

Whatever she's done to herself, it's handy. If she's gone, I'm away. I head for the door.

'Hold! Watch where you step with your great blundering feet!'

It's Allison's voice, from near my ankles. I wave some of the smoke away and peer down at Allison's cloak. Bundled in the middle is a fat earthworm. *Allison*.

I crouch down and pick her up gingerly, cradling her with both hands. She pulsates, warm in my hold, and lifts what I reckon is the head part of her. If she had eyes, she'd be giving me proper evils. Still, she can speak so she can probably see me.

I bite as much of my cheeks as I can to keep from pissing myself. She carries on not-looking at me, stiff as a statue, like a teacher waiting for the class to calm down. When I can get it together, I ask her:

'What happened?'

'It is courtesy, little Matty Groves,' she starts, and I want to laugh again given our sizes, 'to inform somebody when you have damaged their personal property, be it accident or malice.'

'Do what?'

'You broke my wand, oaf.'

I remember that horrible crack I heard earlier, in the darkness, and grin.

'Oh. Sorry about my, er, blundering great feet.' *Good one, Matty.*

I hear a tut, and then she nods towards the bookcase.

'A silver wand I was saving for best – go forth and get it for me?'

I shake my head and crouch down, ready to put her back.

'Get real. You'll only turn *me* into a worm. I'd best make a move.'

'No – wait! Prithee, I will do anything you ask if you will only help change me back.'

'Actually anything?'

'You heard me, sir. A witch's promise is never broken. You shall have whatever your heart desires.'

I raise her up again and start over to the bookcase.

'All right. But I have a – a condition. You can't kill me or do any sort of hocus pocus bullshit on me if I get your wand for you.'

She nods, but it's more of a wormy headbang.

'Yes, yes, done!'

'And you'll help me find Sandy. No ifs or buts or mucking about, right?'

'Very well – now get it!'

I scan the shelves, grabbing the wand from the very top one, and offer it to her. She stares straight back at me. I've missed something here.

'Hold it t'ward me, fool.'

'Oh! Right, yeah, hands would be useful.'

I hold her up in front of me and pull my wand arm back like I'm about to fire an arrow. I try to aim it at her, but it's shaking all the same.

'Very good, sir – *scealu gáste.*'

The wand vibrates in my hand like a medieval dildo – not that I'm in the habit of handling them – and goes red hot. I don't think I can hold it much longer.

Everything goes white as something cracks from the end. I drop Allison and stumble backwards, my wand arm tingling. This thing's got serious power.

When my eyes adjust, white spots gradually disappearing, I see Allison scrambling to her feet. She's got absolutely nothing on. Christ, where do you even *look*? My face catches fire because I've just seen her tits bouncing gently under her hair. They're not too saggy for a middle-aged witch, really. In fact, she's got a cracking body for an older bird – proper hourglass. But she's striding over to me, so I try and look at the floor before I see too much. Too late – she times the walk wrong, so I see all she's got to offer under her spare tyre. I figure a Brazilian isn't exactly top of a witch's to-do list. She snatches the wand off me.

'Allison – you're naked,' I mumble. *Twat. Well done, Captain Obvious.* But what else can I say? Somehow what I've just seen is more disturbing than the worm ever was.

'Come – you behave as though had never seen a cuckoo's nest before.'

Well, that's a new word for it. I hear a rustling sound and when I think it's safe; I look up and Allison's clothed once more, one hand on the cauldron drumming her fingers and the other on her hip. She's waiting for me to say something.

'So, erm… about Sandy?'

'You knew me, Groves. You knew my name. How?'

I bristle.

'Well, you knew *mine*!'

'A witch makes it her business to know who's broken into their home. She has her ways.'

I don't fancy telling her that I didn't break in, that her crow practically invited me, and her building swallowed me, but I'm coming close. I clench my fist.

'Back home – they wrote a song about you. You're a myth, I suppose.' Who knows? Sandy's the expert. 'A folk tale. But you should be *fiction*. Just the fact you're here, in front of me, talking to me – it's bollocks!'

She shrugs.

'Many believe in sacred texts – is that also… "bollocks"?'

I feel my mouth drop open.

'You can't say that!'

She pouts.

'Wherefore can I not?'

'You'll have the PC mob after you.'

She shakes her head, obviously not knowing or caring what that is. But then why should she? If I've gone back in time, there are bound to be some old-school ways of thinking.

'Regardless, I am as real as this tower. And I made thee a promise. So, let us look for this Sandy while you… bring me up to speed, I think you say. Prithee, spit in here.'

She pats her hand on the cauldron's lip. I don't question it, just wiggle my mouth around, trying to get some spit up, and aim for the bubbling liquid. I try and do it like I'm hard and spit all the time because I'm a guy and that's what real guys are meant to do. Half makes it in the cauldron, but the rest dribbles down my chin. *Well, you can't win them all*, I think, wiping my mouth with my hand.

Allison stirs the concoction with the broken wand as I explain everything that's happened. How I'm not sure what exactly *did* happen. Sandy sang this song and then got sucked into this hole and I just went after her and now I don't know where she went or even where I am.

'Kent,' says Allison, waving an arm over the liquid like she's mixing on an epic deck. 'We're in Kent.'

'Bollocks are we.' There's no way we're home. I stare at her, and she stares back.

'Things are not always as plain as you believe, Groves.'

I wish she'd use my first name.

'And do you remember the words of this song?'

She's got me there. I sit down on a wooden stool, near the bookcase.

'Not word for word, not the new bit. All I know is it was talking about bringing some woman back from the dead. Bit morbid, really.'

Allison hangs over the cauldron, as though she's watching something exciting. Her eyes are moving like she's watching a film.

'A noblewoman?' She asks, her tone changing. The hairs all over me stand up as I realise she might actually know what's up.

'Yes, I think so. Lady –'

'*Donald.*' Allison inhales deeply and for the first time I think I see genuine fear in her face. I go cold all over and wish I could rewind this last half-hour. Allison bites her lip and puts her hands on my shoulders.

'Hark, Matty.' *Finally.* 'I know where Sandy is. Lord Donald has her.'

He can't. He's another folk character, confined to the world of weird old-style music. But then I'm speaking to one, plain as day.

'Do you know where he is? I'll–'

Allison shakes me.

'Nay, you must *listen*, sir. Lord Donald is a fiend. A villain, a scoundrel.'

'Sounds nasty,' I concur.

'He is evil.' *Bit rich, coming from a witch.* 'He possesses power far greater than mine, and he will only use it maliciously.'

I bristle, my balls finally materialising.

'He'd better not hurt Sand.'

'He will not – *cannot* – harm her yet.'

'*Yet?*'

9
Matty

I didn't realise Allison's gaff was so close to the sea. Still, here we are walking along the cliffs that look suspiciously like the Downs. It's nothing but grass one side, and a chalky drop into the drink the other. Allison reckons this coastal route is the quickest way to King Henry's castle. We'll see it coming, and we won't get lost. Better, we might come across someone who'll give us a lift. I'm still hoping. I'm cold where the salty winds keep stabbing me and pissed off because my feet are starting to hurt. And I'm knackered. We were up at the crack of dawn and, funnily enough, it's hard to sleep in a witch's tower – it's draughty, and there's a severe lack of bedding. And beds.

We talked about it last night. Allison reckons that going to the king's court is our best bet at finding Donald, seeing as he is actually a genuine lord. He'll be there on business, or somebody will know where he is. Either way, Allison said we need to get to him before he can spill Sandy's blood and that's made me anxious, to say the least. I don't know how she knows all this – I figure she saw it in the cauldron yesterday, that's how she got Donald's name as well. The wanker. He needs to kill Sand; and using some magical bull, her blood will be able to bring back his dead wife. Exactly as that stupid song in that stupid book said. Bloody hell, why did I have to be a div and make a thing out of it? Why didn't I just bite my tongue and agree with Sandy?

That's not the only thing that's worrying me. I'm still trying to work out where I am. Everything feels like we've rewound a few centuries, but Allison reckons it is today – the present.

'So, run this by me again,' I say, wanting to get it drummed into my thick head. 'We're still in England?'

'We are,' Allison says.

'But it's different to *my* England,' I start. She tuts. 'I've gone back in time?'

'No. The England we walk in is timeless. It is the *spell*, lad,' she says, irritably. 'Donald's wife died in this time, and it is to this time Sandy has been brought. How you passed through continues to baffle me.' *Bloody cheek.*

'I still don't get it.' I must sound like a whiny brat, but like I'm bothered.

'I'll not explain it again.'

'But if you'd only say "oh, it's another dimension". Or "why yes, Matty, this *is* a parallel world", I'd be happy.'

'You could not comprehend it! There are many layers 'pon this earth, the *one* earth. They sit not above one another, but meld together. Have you not seen something out of the corner of your eye before? A phantom, a blur?'

I shrug.

'Well, yeah.'

'Then the chances are you've seen someone going about

their business in another layer. It would not surprise me if this is how the songs get out – the fabric is worn thin in places.'

I stop dead.

'Fabric? Like a space-time fabric or some shit?'

'Certainly.' It almost sounds like a question, and she looks at me like she's daring me to say something before dropkicking me over the cliffs. I kick a stone over the edge.

'Well, you might've said earlier – that's all. Christ, where's this *castle*?'

There's nothing but grass-topped cliffs ahead. Allison's all right, levitating along in her invisible bubble so the wind doesn't get to her, but I'm getting fed up.

'Don't you do like a teleporting spell or something?'

'I am but a *witch*, Matty. I cannot perform miracles.'

After a bit, Allison cups a hand above her eyes and squints.

'I think there may be two gentlemen, up ahead – I am certain they would ease your mind.'

Sure enough, there are two black spots a few hundred feet away, gradually becoming silhouettes, and then actual people. When they're in earshot, I smile and wave at them. And holler the only olde-worlde greeting I can think of.

'Ho, there!'

Allison drops out of her bubble like a stuffed toy out of a grabber machine and shoves me.

'Ho? *Ho?*'

I take my hand down quick as you like.

'Isn't that how you greet people in Old England?' That's what I've decided to call it, now. I thought about it earlier on and it kind of stuck.

'What's wrong with "good morning"?' she says – through gritted, false-smiling teeth because she's trying to be civil, too.

It doesn't matter, because the blokes stop and greet us, anyway. They're dressed like the sailors in the old black-and-white films Sandy likes, loose white shirts with the sleeves rolled up and trousers that look eye-wateringly tight. One's a real mardy arse, with a face like someone's shoved a turd under his nose, and arms crossed. The smaller one seems all right, smiling widely, even though he's got two swords tucked in his belt. The way his hair's blowing about in the wind and his power stance make him look like a cocky school kid trying to impress a bird or get into a bar. Then as they come nearer, I twig it's not actually a bloke at all, but a woman with short hair. She sticks a filthy hand out, and nearly breaks my fingers when I grab it. She shakes my hand like she's trying to get the last dregs of ketchup out of the bottle.

'I wonder,' I start, then give up because I can't talk properly at the best of times let alone try and sound Old English *and* polite. 'Is this the way to King Henry's castle?'

'Your efforts are wasted if you would ask this one, sir,' the woman pipes up, nudging Mardy. 'He's a very fool in matters of navigation.'

'I escaped *thee*,' Mardy retorts.

'Aye, but not as long as you would have had.' She prods a finger into his chest, and I wince just thinking about the strength in her hands. That'd have to cane on his bony body.

Allison claps her hands. Nobody wants a part in someone else's domestic.

'Gentlemen, *please*!'

Gentlemen? Then Allison's not aware that the little one's a bird. Can she really be that thick? All the while I'm wondering how the hell someone can get confused over something so obvious, the arguing escalates. Then I hear Mardy accuse the bird of something interesting.

'... To expose yourself, before all those men – and midst the battle!'

'And again, 'twas but the wind, you cloth-eared yellow belly!'

Mardy scowls.

'Well, we both know all you sought of me was at the bottom of my belly.'

'From whence comes this conceit? If I sought anything of thee, it is lost!' She snaps.

Nah. I think we'd be better off out of these two's hair. I try to catch Allison's eye, hoping she'll twig, and we can both make a move, but she's slipped between the pair of them, hands on each of their shoulders. She's looking Mardy up and down, trying to decide on something, pouting her lips in deliberation. Then she leans into the woman, mouth at her ear and tits in her shoulder. I was right; she hasn't twigged – but then why would she? This place is starting to make more sense as we crack on, and I'm guessing that tomboys aren't the norm here like they are at home. I doubt people have ever even seen one.

'I bet *you've* something and a half at the bottom of your belly, son,' says Allison. I stick a hand to my mouth – half to keep from creasing up, and half in disbelief. You wouldn't even try something like that if you were totally wankered.

'What a handsome young man you are.' Allison's stroking

this bird's hair now, but she's making no attempt to stop her, just kind of taking it. I don't fancy putting Allison right. Common sense is screaming at me not to embarrass a witch.

Mardy taps a finger on Allison's shoulder.

'I say, do you mind?'

'Not really,' Allison says, blankly. 'Dost thou?'

'As a matter of fact, I dost. *Do*,' he says, red-faced. Then he puts his fists up – terrific, Allison's libido is going to get the pair of us killed. I brace myself, wondering who will be the first one into the sea. Allison tuts, as though it's a minor inconvenience, and slides a hand into her cloak. She whips her wand out, and as soon as Mardy claps eyes on it, he drops his fists. All the colour in his face goes walkies, too. The woman laughs her head off and gently puts a hand on Allison's own – not even scared of possible witchy repercussions.

'Good lady, I fear your sentiments are wasted on me. I am a woman – Sarah-Jane Taylor, at thy service.' She bows like she might be on stage and Allison's face just about drops.

'What a disappointment,' Allison huffs, staring at Sarah-Jane's hint of boob.

'No – here the disappointment stands!' Sarah-Jane elbows Mardy, who nearly goes flying. Then he tugs his shirt slightly out of his swashbuckler's strides.

'They call me *Bold* William Taylor.' He sniffs, and shoots Sarah-Jane daggers, daring her to question it. With the way he's been acting, she'd have every right to. There's no doubt about these two, now – I know their bloody history. Yet another stupid song from The Groveses back catalogue, just like *Allison Gross* – Sandy'd have a field day here. I really hope this isn't going to be a pattern.

'And this *woman*,' William spits, pointing at Sarah-Jane, 'impersonated a seaman to sail halfway about the world and kill my lady!'

Sarah-Jane's chest puffs up indignantly and she thrusts herself into him. From behind, she's the image of little man syndrome.

'I be your *wife*! I am your *only* lady.'

'Oh, you two would be *brilliant* on *Jeremy Kyle*.' It just comes out of me, and everyone stares.

'Of which Jeremy do you speak? Is he a lord?' William asks. He does it blankly, seriously, and I can't hack it anymore.

'Look, *is* this the way to Henry's castle? Because I'm not being funny, but I'm up to here with your poxy marital problems when I've got my own shit to deal with!'

It's horrible, and I know it going by the disapproving mum look Allison's giving me. But time's getting on, and I don't know how much of it Sandy's got left. William grumbles a bit, but Sarah-Jane smiles at me – kindly, like she gets it. Then she turns to her husband-not-husband.

'It appears that fortune would favour you, William – the clink can wait.'

She claps a hand on his shoulder and forces him around to face the way they came. Then she beams at us and hooks a thumb over her shoulder.

'Come, then – the castle is two miles yonder.'

I find my voice again.

'Hang on, are you showing us the way?'

'Of course,' Sarah-Jane says, starting to walk.

'Oh brilliant, cheers!' I follow her, and Allison puts her wand away.

William chokes with disbelief.

'Now, look you here, Sarah–'

'No, look *you* here,' Sarah-Jane butts in, pressing a finger into his bony chest. 'We need not like one another, but we have agreed to help the boy –'

'*You* agreed,' he mutters.

'And help him we shall.' She sniffs. 'Besides, his vestments amuse me.'

'Sorry, my *what* amuse you?' I spit out.

Allison grabs my arm in a death-grip and shakes her head, silently telling me not to answer back. Not that Sarah-Jane minds my asking.

'Vestments – garments. *Apparel*,' she sighs, finally getting a word I understand.

'All right, all right – swallow a dictionary, did you?' Then I think what a bloody cheek it was to take the piss out of my clobber when I've only got my t-shirt and jeans on. If anything, I'm the one that should be able to laugh about ye olde-worlde cross-dressing. Still, I keep my mouth shut because I think that tiny brown speck in the distance is a castle, and it's nice to have people willing to help me – no, *us*.

10
Sandy

'Coming a-milking with us later, m'lady?'

It's a voice I haven't heard before. I can only see the girl's feet from here at ground level – filthy, unfamiliar wooden clogs, and I don't really want anyone talking to me. My back's hurting. My knees are hurting. I'm hot, and everything's wet where I'm scrubbing the floor. Aswell as all that, they've taken the dog away from me, and I don't know where they've put him. Or if he's even all right. I'm just pissed off and wish everyone would leave me alone to fume. But there's something in the voice, like an echo of kindness, that makes me chuck my brush down and heave myself up.

The girl in the clogs can't be much older than me, but she's holding herself like a middle-aged woman, hand on her hip and her whole being sagging as though she's hard-pressed. She's smiling, but I wish she wouldn't – the teeth she's showing off are either yellow or missing. I have to smile myself, though – this is the first proper smile anyone here's shown me.

'I thought milking was done in the morning?' I ask her. Because I thought that was always the order of the day, even back home.

'Aye. But this milking can't be done with cows, m'lady,' she says, like she's bringing me in on a secret plot. I have a bit of a think and then I realise that milking must be code – milkmaids and ploughboys are always at it like rabbits in folksong. Well, some things never change – people will always want to get their end away.

'By the stables,' she tells me. 'You shall find Abigail and me there when the thrush starts singing.'

Thrush. Think, Sand, think, that's…

'That's night time, right?'

'Aye, m'lady.'

I wince.

'What's with this "m'lady" malarkey? Call me Sandy, yeah?'

She giggles at that.

'All right, Sandy. I'm Ellyn.'

I couldn't give a toss what her name is, really. Much as it'd be nice if we could be friends, it's not important if I'm not going to be hanging around. I'm not intending to.

This Donald's some sort of idiot, I think to myself as I return to the bucket. He could have locked me up or anything – but having me work in the kitchen, well, that's his own bloody fault for not thinking it through.

When the thrush starts singing, us girls will be out of the grounds. And I'll be well away.

11

Matty

When we get to the castle, the drawbridge is down, but there's nobody about. It's a grand affair, and I'm not surprised that it looks familiar to me. I reckon that some of the buildings must be shared across those worldly layers that Allison was chatting about. Sandy's probably dragged me around this place on one of our painfully educational days out. I wish she was here with me now, getting all excited and telling me the names of all the different parts, instead of my current wacky entourage.

'I like this not. Matty, this is not proper,' Allison says. I'm halfway across the drawbridge, but she and the two Taylors have stopped dead on the other side of the moat. I don't think witches are meant to be scared, or have manners, or do any of the things that normal people do, but just like everything in this place, Allison continues to surprise me. I don't know what she's on about, when it was her bloody idea to come here. The quicker we can get in and out, the closer I'll be to finding Sandy. I'll break in if I have to. It can't be any harder than breaking into a Ford Fiesta round the back of the local shops.

This is just a massive, stone Fiesta, with better returns than the manky old stereo you can flog to the boy racers in your class. And no noisy alarms to give the game away. It'd be a piece of piss. Only Allison's still whinging on about manners.

'Matty, hold,' she says.

I shrug.

'Why? We're here, so let's go in.'

Allison shakes her head.

'You comprehend not.'

'Aye, she's right,' Sarah-Jane agrees, and gestures towards the castle. 'Look about you – no guards, yonder, for to man the gate. This is asking for trouble.'

William's actually smiling – either with relief or just being the smug git he is – and pats Sarah-Jane on the shoulder.

'So, you do have some sense within you after all, woman.' I twig her cringe. 'Matty,' he continues, giving me the titchiest of bows. 'We have brought you to the castle, true to our word. Now we must depart. Good day to you.' He grabs Sarah-Jane's wrist, like an angry parent trying to drag their kid that's acting up away, but she shakes him off.

'Who are "we"?' She spits at him. '*I'll* leave them not.'

William takes a deep breath like an asthmatic trying to get the air.

'You will do as I say. You are my *wife*.'

There's no way he can get away with saying something like that. Even if this place is their present day, that's just way too backward. I almost want to say something, but Sarah-Jane beats me to it.

'So now I be your wife – as it suits you! Honestly.' She

glares at him, daring him to have another pop. I know the look – it was the same one my mum used to give my dad when she was itching for the row to carry on. And this stupid git only bites.

'Well?' William demands. 'Shall we take our leave?'

'Take what you will – only take this with you!' Then she lamps him one, copping him right on the chin. There's enough force there to send him flying. He doesn't half deserve it, but that's bound to cane. 'And let that be a lesson. Egad, I know not what I saw in you!'

Allison's tittering, her hand up in front of her face, and that really winds him up. I can't laugh, though. He strikes me as that much of a dick that he wouldn't hesitate to hit one of the women, and I'm ready to have him if he does. But he doesn't. Instead, he gets to his feet slowly. His mouth's full of blood and his words come out all wet and slobbering.

'Fine – go with the witch and the queerly attired boy if you must. I wash my hands of you, Sarah-Jane Taylor!'

She laughs.

'Fool, where would you go? You're a wanted man, William – remember that!'

He storms off, hollering to the winds.

''Tis no concern of thine! Get you back to your new allies!'

He's got a point, it's none of her business and to be honest she's got to be well rid of him. Their *history*, though. She's killed for him, so the song goes. That's got to take it out of you. Still, I know I'd do the same for Sand – though I really hope things don't get to that stage.

'Be you well?' Allison asks Sarah-Jane. Silly cow, she's

obviously not. Her eyes are glazing over, and she seems to be trembling. Yet she still puts on one of those fronts, sucking it up and playing hard.

'It matters not,' Sarah-Jane spits. Then she strides on, over the drawbridge.

When we're through the gatehouse, the bailey's empty and I'm not sure it's meant to be. It's that courtyard part of the castle, and I only know the name because Sandy bends my earhole with all the proper names and guidebook trivia when we go on our days out. She also said something about it being the heart of a castle where the horses are kept, the tradesmen work, all that kind of thing. The stables are over to one side, sure enough, because there's a smell of shit in the air, and there are tools and carts scattered all around. But that's all. There's no sign of human life, apart from Sarah-Jane, next to me, and Allison, just hanging back.

'This displeases me greatly,' Allison mutters, looking all around like a jumpy animal. 'You should both know better.'

That does it. I'm sick of being treated like a kid who doesn't know anything. I'm from now, which isn't then-now, it's technically the future, and I know more than anyone in this stupid time warp. I *have* to. So, I muster all the swag I've got. You've got to have swag, whatever that is, when you've got the ultimate comeback. Only I never get a chance to say it.

'Intruders!'

Oh, they can bugger *right* off – seriously? Somewhere up on the battlements there's military-style stamping on stone, and I know that's our cue to leave. But we're screwed. The drawbridge is being raised. Allison's glaring at it and mumbling some nonsense words under her breath, but if it's a spell, it's having no effect. Guess we're taking on soldiers now.

We're lucky that despite the noise they made, there's only three of them as they storm towards us. They're not exactly prime candidates either, even if they are pointing huge, spear-like polearms at us. One looks like he's struggling to hold his glaive up, let alone aim it, and one's got a face like a radish, like he's been on too much gatter. The only one who looks like he might be capable of doing anything to us seems to be their leader, and even he's carrying an extra sack of spuds in his breastplate. He points his longsword at me and it's that impressive that I don't focus on the blade. It's that shiny gold cross-guard that's got me. He weighs me up like a fat chicken might, his head is to one side and he's eyeing me suspiciously.

'State thy business.'

Play it cool. Don't tell him too much.

'I want to see King Henry.'

His beard twists up to one side, and he nudges Radish with his elbow.

'A blind man should like to *see* King Henry, boy.'

The soldiers crack up at that awful joke. I don't think I can take it. Not dad jokes. I look at Allison and nod towards the place where she keeps her wand. If only she'd take it out and zap them, we'd be laughing. But she only shakes her head and puts her fingers to her mouth and makes a sort of speaking motion. *Got it.* Match their mouth, not their might.

'I much desire to speak with him, then.' I beam, impressed with my own, superior Middle-Earth joke. It all feels a bit Tolkien to me, anyway, this place. And at least the soldiers seem to understand me, because they've stopped laughing. We might get somewhere after all. I turn to Sarah-Jane for approval, but she's rubbing at the back of her neck so hard it looks like what little hair she's got will come away. *What have I done?*

'Such audacity can only mean you are an enemy of the king,' says Spuds. 'Arrest them.'

'What?' I hold my hands up, because I think that's what you're meant to do when hostile bastards come after you. 'No, I only want to know where I can find Lord Donald.'

I think someone behind me just groaned. *You bloody numb-nuts.*

'Allies of Donald – kill them!'

Before I know what's happening, the men advance, bills pushed out ready to impale us. I clench my eyes shut and grit my teeth. *This is it. I'm sorry, Sand.*

Something's thrust into my chest, but it's not sharp.

'Here,' someone instructs.

I open my eyes and take the rusty old broadsword that Sarah-Jane's bunged at me. She's bouncing up and down on her toes like she's itching for aggro, her own sword dancing in her hand.

'And what d'you expect me to do with this?' *Because how the hell am I meant to know how to use a sword when I can't even talk to people?*

'Well, if you want it not…'

I bristle and hug it to my chest.

'No, I want it.'

'For Jove's sake, be silenced!' Allison yells. She steps forward and with a garnet flash from her wand, Spuds's sword is smacked out of his hand and flies across the bailey. It impales a pile of sacks full of veggies, and rests erect like a comedy sword in the stone. Spuds stands there blinking for a while, his glove steaming, while his cronies cower like a pair of lost dogs.

One of them stage-whispers:

'Be she a witch?'

'What think you, man?' Spuds snaps, coming to his senses. 'Kill her!'

Radish and The Struggler are back in action and coming at us tenfold. Spuds has run for his sword, so I sprint off after him, the sounds of clashing metal and unearthly zapping ringing in my ears. Something tells me that the birds will be all right without me for the minute.

'Sir – this lad's very good!' Shouts the Struggler, apparently struggling with Sarah-Jane.

I swear I hear her groan from across the courtyard, but I don't have time to look. Spuds is trying to wrench his sword out of the sack. It can't be that hard to get out, surely, but he looks like he's having a job with his face all sweaty and pulling with all his might.

'Oh no you don't, mate!' I've got my own sword still, but it doesn't seem right to use it when he's defenceless. Sandy would probably tell me that's bollocks and to look out for number one, but she's not here and I wouldn't even know where to start, anyway. So I drop the sword and jump on his back. The shock, or the weight of me, or possibly both forces him back and he starts batting at my arms.

'Matty!'

That sounds like Allison. I've got my hands clamped over Spuds' face, so he can't see. He keeps spinning me around and trying to shake me off all at once. Then he stops and starts clawing at my arms again, and I clap eyes on Allison backing away from Radish, who's swinging his glaive at her for all he's worth.

'Can't you zap him?' I yell.

'It takes great skill to 'zap' when one is also dodging blows – you try it!' As if to show me, she shoots off a few balls of fire between swings, but they zip straight past Radish and disintegrate in the air.

'All right keep your hair on!'

The *clang-clash-schwing*ing of metal and cocky cries lets me know that Sarah-Jane's all right for the minute, but if I can only help Allison, we might have a chance. I pull Spuds' helmet off and, not knowing what else to do because I don't fancy trying to gouge his eyes out, I bite his ear. Nothing comes off in my mouth, thank God, but it's enough to make him shout in pain and double over on the ground. I toe him a few times to buy some time before grabbing my sword and running towards Allison, and Radish going at her. She sends turquoise fire Radish's way, but it misses and shoots between his legs. It's heading for me.

I dive. The fire misses my feet by inches. It plunges into the pile of sacks, but instead of burning, the whole thing freezes. The ice crackles upwards, caking the pile. It works its way up the blade of the sword, which Spuds has limped over to and grabbed, before shattering. The sword goes with it, and I see Spuds cursing at the mound of glittering steel dust in his hands.

Sarah-Jane hollers from near the drawbridge.

'Well done, that witch!'

I don't know how she's done it, but she's managed to dangle the Struggler from his own glaive, the head buried in the wood. *Two down, one to go.*

I can't get over what comes next. There's a cart behind Allison, a busted old wooden thing that she's backed herself into. Only instead of bumping into it like any normal person, she rolls over the thing like some police officer over a car bonnet, and slides underneath. She pokes her wand out between the spokes of a wheel, and I think she's going to do the clever thing and zap Radish, only her aim's way off. It seems to be pointing at me and I could kick myself if this was all some sort of cunning witchy conspiracy plan.

'*Bærnap tanede!*'

The heat from the orange stream exploding out is intense, but it flies right between my legs and into the feet of Spuds. *Shit*. He was coming at me from behind. She's had my back all along, and even with Radish hacking into the wood on top of her, she was looking out for me. I feel a right tool now and even looking at Spuds' feet on fire doesn't cheer me up.

'I'm on fire! Oh, hell! Do something!' He cries, stamping his feet and fanning at the flames. Radish drops his weapon and comes over to see what all the fuss is about. Sarah-Jane follows, one hand on the Struggler's shoulder and the other behind him, detaining his struggling hands. Christ, she's not even breaking a sweat. Allison composes herself, like a proper lady, picking herself up from under the cart and dusting herself down.

'Oh hush, you great maiden's mantle,' she demands, cool as you like. 'I shall put you out if you'll not kill us.'

Spuds is nearly in tears now. The fire's not spreading like I'd expect it to and can't be hurting him too badly because he's not even murmuring. I wonder if Allison can control the intensity of it, if this is just an illusion to trash him.

'For the love of Jove – *please*!' He cries.

'Better. *Gerín*.' With a flick of her wrist, the wand goes limp in her hand, like a noodle before water comes gushing out like a hose. It half drowns Spuds and puts the fire out, but there's no smoke or anything.

'That was not so difficult, was it?' Allison's tone reminds me of someone telling a kid to apologise.

'No, my hag– my *lady*.' He pouts.

'Now, this all could have been avoided if you had only let the boy *speak*,' Allison carries on, grabbing onto me. 'There's naught can be settled with swords that cannot be settled with words more imminently.'

'Well, *I* enjoyed myself,' huffs Sarah-Jane, shoving her prisoner away from her. Allison frowns and rubs at her forehead as if she's a mum on the verge of getting up to here with her kids' shit wherever "here" actually is. I think it varies from mum to mum, but it's generally eye-level.

I clear my throat and rest my sword on my shoulders. 'So, are you gonna take us to Henry or what?'

It's a start. Spuds grabs his helmet from the floor and donks it on his head before giving us the slightest of nods.

'This way.'

12
Matty

They took us through the keep and down some spiral steps that were so steep, narrow and worn that I had to hold on to the wall and go slow, making sure both of my shaky feet were planted firmly. Seriously, what is it with this place? It's like they've got major beef with banisters or something. Even a rope or some sort of handholds would have done, and not a sheer drop. I got the mickey taken right out of me by Sarah-Jane, who was up my back the whole time, but I'd rather be called a "yellow-bellied cumber-world" multiple times than smash my head open.

Now, on flat ground, we're going along some passageway that smells of old roast dinners and smoke. It's hot, but that'll be the torches on the wall between the tapestries. And the worry. I know we must be in some kind of danger despite our little truce, but now all I can think of is how brave these people are to keep naked flames burning next to hanging fabric. Sarah-Jane is whistling some little tune behind me, breaking up the echo of our footsteps. I think I recognise it. Allison's silent, with only the swish of her cloak against the stone floor reminding me that she's behind me as we head towards impending doom.

We finally stop in front of some hefty wooden doors. Spuds bangs his fist against the wood three times. One of them opens a crack, and a sour-faced old git slithers through. Everything about him is long – long nose, long chin, long scowl. He looks me up and down before nodding at Spuds and pushing the doors open.

'You will kneel before his majesty,' he gums at me before stepping aside to let us through.

Christ, I'm not prepared for this. I didn't expect we'd be seeing the actual king, or having an audience with him, or whatever the right phrase is for it. What do you say to a king? Do you speak first, or do you wait for him to say something to you? What do you call him? These are the things you'd be better off learning at school. The tiny, practical, historically accurate things, just so you don't make a complete twat of yourself when you find yourself living in the almost-past. Not all of the political and battle stuff and dates get repeated regardless of what textbook you look at.

'Take courage, Matty,' Sarah-Jane whispers. My head's getting swallowed into my shoulders. I feel more nervous now than about anything that's happened so far. 'Rarely does the king grant audience to the common man in haste.' *Right. Cheers for that, I feel way better now.*

We follow Spuds into a great big hall, and it's so quiet that I find myself taking extra special care to breathe quietly. Until my breathing becomes so shallow that I choke and break out into coughing fit central. Feeling a right tit, Allison thumps me on the back and my eyes water. Through the tears, I can tell we're interrupting something. Something *big*. Mega-long tables line the longer sides of the room, and the one at the furthest end. About fifty different heads, all wearing floppy hats and pointy hennins turn in their seats, away from piles of food. Shit, I think we're interrupting their lunch.

'Forgive the disturbance, my liege,' Spuds begins, shuffling forward and going down on one knee in a dramatic bow.

'Come, Dimsby,' a voice thunders. 'What ails you? Say your piece, then get you to the kitchen and tell the cook to ease up, ere she make a pig of me – ha!'

My eyes have stopped streaming, and I see Spuds – no, Dimsby – is still hunched over in front of a big buff bloke, rigged out in all the colours you can think of and dripping in gold that'd make a rapper jealous. He's got ginger hair cocked up like he's slept funny, and a matching beard that, properly groomed, could let him pass off as a footballer or ironic East Londoner. I get that this is the king, but he seems like a sound bloke. I'm even getting the feeling, like I did with the others, that I've had some dealings with him before, in the normal world. His face looks so familiar, and it's eating away at my brain trying to think where I've seen him. He fidgets in his seat and nods towards us.

'What are these?' He asks, his eyes lighting up. If it was Christmas, he'd be the kid with the shiny new RC car he'd begged for, and his parents actually remembered to buy batteries.

'My liege – two gentlemen and a witch desire to speak with you.'

'That'll do, Dimsby,' Henry says, waving him away because all these lords and ladies have started whispering amongst themselves at the very mention of a witch. Dimsby hurries off somewhere towards the back of the hall, taking his cronies with him, and leaving me and the girls completely at this bloke's mercy.

'Come then, let's have you. What is it you want?'

Here we go, then. Don't balls this one up, mate.

'My name is Matty Groves, sire – can I say that? Sire, I mean?'

The corners of his mouth turn up and he looks me up and down like he's trying to work me out, but he nods slowly. Kindly. Perhaps this'll be all right.

'Well, I was hoping you'd be able to tell me where I can find Lord Donald.'

I think that was the wrong way to word it. I don't know what the bloke's deal is, but everyone around the tables start whispering amongst themselves and giving me some filthy looks. I swallow hard when I clock Henry's hand screwing up the table runner.

'That rotten knave! I hope you seek him out to kill him?'

'I don't want to kill anyone!' I protest. 'Christ, people here are so quick to judge.'

'Be you his ally, then?' Henry asks, leaning forward and moving his hand slowly down towards his side. *Please – no more swords, not today.*

'No, sir. He's… taken something very dear to me.' I wince at how pants that sounds. The king puts his hand back on the table and starts fiddling with his goblet. I don't really know what more I can say without sounding like a loser or embarrassing myself, or both. Allison rustles up behind me – ready to help, I think. I hope. She takes a breath near my ear like she's going to start whispering to me.

Henry slams a hand on the table, and seventy-five percent of the room jumps.

'What say you to Groves, hag?'

'Well, really!' She huffs. 'That's not at all kind, sir.'

'You are a witch, are you not?'

'Aye, but we are not all warts and toads, my lord.' She catches mine and Sarah-Jane's eyes and curtsies in front of the king, bending as low as she can go, really taking the piss. Not that he notices. He settles back in his chair and grins.

'Show us some magic, then. Go on.'

Allison takes her wand out and taps it on the heel of her shoe.

'Sorry,' I protest, 'wasn't this about me?'

I feel Sarah-Jane's hands on my shoulders.

'Aye, let him say his piece.'

'Button it, lad!' Dimsby's voice echoes dangerously from the other side of the hall.

'Oh, honestly!' She spits, spinning around to give him the deadliest of death stares. 'I. Am. A. Woman!' With that, she smacks the hilt of her sword twice into her chest, breast by breast, and waits for an answer as Dimsby, and probably the rest of the court, stare at her parts.

'Be you a heretic, then?' Dimsby tries.

'I give up!' She throws her hands in the air and turns away, crossing her arms and getting right narky.

'Enough!' Henry stands and puts a hand to his hip in a kind of power stance. It's the stance that's a silent command to everyone in the room not to move, or even breathe loudly, unless you want to end up on the chopping block. It's the stance you see in every single portrait of the guy. Everyone's hushed up, but inside I'm screaming. I know what Henry we're standing in front of. Stick a floppy hat on him and pad him out a bit and he'd be the spit of his older self in some of the paintings I've seen. This is Henry VIII, and I call bullshit on Allison's insistence that this is the present day and I'm going to have to have a word or something later because what the actual hell?

'I believe your cause is true, Groves. Donald is a beast and has caused me naught but headache.'

'Sure, his majesty resides here but temporarily with the intention to take back half of Kent from him!' Dimsby hollers.

'Silence, you loose-lipped codpiece!'

I shrink back, but his face completely changes as he sits down again. It shifts from red and murderous to pale and best-mate-like.

'Now, Groves, I shall gladly help you in your quest to retrieve your –?'

'Sandy – she's my girlfriend.'

'Ho, so it be a *maiden*! Any man would think you incapable!'

My ears go tinnitus on me and I feel my face flush. There are a few sniggers around the hall.

'What d'you mean by that?'

'It's all in jest, Groves. Now, I help those that help me. What services can the three of you offer my court? Prove thy worth and you shall have my aid.'

Shit, he's got me there. This is every single part-time job interview I've ever had rolled into one, complete with cold sweats. Only this time there's added life-or-death stakes. This bloke's out to screw me right over because I'm useless and I always will be.

'Well?'

It's not just him. Everyone in the hall is staring at me. All of a sudden, I feel like I'm back at school on a Monday morning, and all the gym wankers are waiting outside the locker room to beat me up, for nothing but wearing my band t-shirts and hanging around with the Weird Girl. I should have stood up to them then, like I need to stand up for myself now. For Sand. But all I do is look desperately at Allison, hoping that telepathy works because in my head I'm begging her to please do something magical and do us all a favour.

For a second, I wonder if it's actually worked. Allison steps forward, wand extended. I don't even laugh when a few people gasp and bristle, ready to run lest ye olde hocus-pocus shit should go down. She breathes on the tip, then draws an invisible figure of eight in front of her, and then to either side of her – one for each table.

Then there are squeals, and the good kind of gasps, as more food appears on the tables, bursting up through the wood itself. There are roasted animals of every size, glazed pigs, mutton, chicken, and even what looks like deer. There are smaller, gamier offerings like crispy rabbit, pheasant and something like tiny chicken which could be either grouse or quail – or both. What do I know about posh banquety grub? There are platefuls of fresh fruit, the reddest of apples, great big bunches of grapes and cherries as big as Ping-pong balls. It's the potatoes that get me, though, massive wooden dishes of greasy roasties piled up high, that twist up out of the wood like a glorious edible drill-bit. My mouth waters and I wish I could just grab a few to be getting on with. Manners stop me from helping myself and my stomach rumbles indignantly.

I turn to Allison.

'So, you can magic up a great big feast for this lot, but you couldn't do me a bed last night? Cheers.'

'Ask not, get not,' Allison hisses at me, her eyes on Henry. He tears off an entire leg from the animal in front of him, and the rest of his guests must take that as the "okay" signal and dig in. He takes a huge bite, grease spilling down into his beard and bits flying out as he chews, and he laughs with a full mouth.

'By Jove, if you will not prove your worth ten times over!' A big chunk narrowly misses Allison, but she stands firm. 'I can think of many uses for you, witch!'

She nods her head and gives another one of her comic curtsies before stepping back.

'I thank you, my *liege*.'

'Boy?'

Now I'm sure it's my turn, but Henry's not even looking at me. He's staring at Sarah-Jane and I wonder how thick you can get because she's even explained it already.

'Me?' Sarah-Jane asks. 'Oh, but I'm—'

Henry rubs at the bridge of his nose, his eyes squeezed up in that "oops" expression.

'Sorry, my dear. You're just so… *convincing*.'

I'm not sure that's something I'd be proud of, but then I don't make a habit of running around in drag. Still, she beams and puts her hand to her sword.

'If it pleases you, my lord,' she says, sliding the blade out of its scabbard, 'my technique be about the best service I can offer.'

'Think thou art a swordsman, girl?'

Swordswoman, I think, then could kick myself because women probably don't even get to play sport in this place.

'Aye,' she says, plain as plain can be.

'I will be privy to this,' Henry decides, then gets to his feet. Shuffling around the table, he looks a lot bigger than he did behind it, and athletic with it. Normally I'd say there's no way someone Sarah-Jane's size will be any match for him – it's like watching one of the skinny lads from the estate go up against a sumo wrestler. Still, you've got to admire her balls – she's got way more than me, and mine are *real*.

They set it all out like a proper duel once Henry's sword's been chucked to him from somewhere. He and Sarah-Jane bow to each other, oh-so-seriously, then get into position. It looks painful, legs bent in an epic lunge that makes your arse stick out, sword touching sword, while the other arm goes over your head as if you're a camp martial arts expert. They hold the position for a little while, giving Allison just enough time to clamp onto my arm and start giving me a one-handed Chinese burn. Then it begins.

13
Matty

I'm shocked when Henry doesn't let Sarah-Jane make the first move. But then, why should he? They spar quickly, quietly. Expertly. So much for the image of that fat Henry VIII who needed a winch to get up the stairs to bed. He's quick, but she's quicker. I really want to cheer her on, but something tells me I'd get lynched.

I feel like I'm under attack as it is, what with Allison screwing my arm up. She's pulling all sorts of anxious faces, all winces and gasps.

'Oh. Do you know how this ends up?' I wonder if witches have future vision. She did manage to see Sandy in that cauldron back at the tower.

'Nay. I can hardly bear it!'

Neither can the court, it seems. Everybody's stopped eating, so this must be as cutting-edge as banquet entertainment gets. There's no sound but the padding of their feet around the hall, and the *swish* and *sching* of their swords. Their faces are pure concentration. Sarah-Jane's tongue even pokes out every now and again, like a kid concentrating on their colouring in. She's that into it that she wouldn't be going over any of the lines. She throws blows every way she can, upwards, downwards, parrying like her life depends on it. Maybe it does. There's nothing to say the king's not a complete nutter and wouldn't skewer her before sportsman's etiquette tells him to stop.

There's a gasp as the fighting gets a bit too close for comfort to the courtiers. Allison's well past putting Chinese burns on me now and is virtually wrenching my arm from its socket. She's watching with the wide-eyed worry of a mother or a lover, too scared to look away. Do witches get scared? It's something I can't work out, seeing as she's been pretty chilled for the twenty-four hours I've known her. Except for that weird clingy shit she pulled in the tower, but then how would anyone react if they only had crows to talk to?

I don't get time to ponder on it. There's clapping, and both swords people have stopped. They're sweating their eyeballs out and bowing to each other, some conclusion having apparently been reached even though no blows have been landed. My guts tighten as Henry lifts a hand to her, but then he grips her shoulder and laughs and everything's all right again.

'By Jove, but thy form does you credit! I could use a girl like you in my ranks – teach the lads a thing or two!'

'I thank thee, sire,' Sarah-Jane says, humbly, before bowing again and stepping back to join us. Allison hugs her to her bosom with some relief as Henry settles at the table.

'Methinks that be two of three,' Henry says. 'And what of thee, Groves? What have you to offer?'

This is it, then. The big moment, and I've still got bugger all to impress him with. I look about – something anything will do. If I only had my phone, I could whip that out, show them all the different apps and amaze them all with its games and music-playing wonder and have done with it.

Music. Shit, that's why I'm here, after all. Ironic or not, I might just be able to tide him over with a song. It's the one thing I can do right.

There's a band of sorts at the other end of the hall, at their own little end of one of the tables. They've got a few instruments, leaning against the wall while they tuck in, but there must be at least one there I could have a crack at.

'Hang about a minute, sire,' I tell Henry.

'I think he means "excuse me",' Allison translates as I give Sarah-Jane my sword for safekeeping. I jog off to their table.

The grumbles and dubious whispers of the crowd don't bother me. I'm in gig mode now – and even though crowds make me nervous, you just learn to brush the whispers off. Sand would know the name of all these instruments; I only know what they look like. There are two big clarinet-like things, a dulcimer whatsit, a drum that is actually a drum, and a few guitar-y things. No, I know the names of these ones – *lutes.*

'Hurry up, Groves!' Bellows Henry.

Lute it is. It can't be *that* much different to a guitar. I pick the biggest one up, the closest in size to my own guitar. One of the beardy blokes at the table opens his mouth to object as I give it a couple of test strums.

'Sorry. I'll bring it back,' I promise.

I walk back towards Henry, quickly working out the key and tuning it up. Then I test a few notes, fingers up and down the fretboard. Then eventually chords. Christ, it's *so* much like a guitar. *Sorted*.

'Well?' Henry's drumming his fingers now.

CHUG-A-CHUNGGGG. The chord seems to buzz through the hall, and everyone in it. There are a few squeals, "oh"s, and hands clamping over ears, but mostly there's curiosity. Especially from Henry. He's leaning forward in his seat, eyes about to pop straight out of his head with enthusiasm. Or shock. It's hard for me to tell with most people. I carry on regardless.

I don't think to play anything in particular. It just sort of comes out, like the way you find yourself back at the *Smoke On The Water* riff when you're only meant to be sodding about. It's not folk I play, either – this is *my* time, not Sandy's, and I've got to make an impression. What started as mindless plucking has suddenly manifested into a melody from a heavy metal floor filler back home.

Well, you'd never expect to see head-banging hennins, but there are plenty of the ladies' fair at it as the band pick it up and offer backing. Lords too, rocking out as best they can. These people don't know the music, but they *get* it. I haven't felt like my music has reached people in such a way before, that they actually *enjoy* it. Playing the folk was always Sandy's department, and I was always just the guy that backed her. She'd gauge a response to *her* music in *her* way, and I'd just get on with it. Now, I'm gauging a response in *my* way, and it's bloody fantastic. It feels good, making people feel good.

It's mad how fast the band all picked it up, but it just seems to work – whether it's Allison's doing, I don't know – but the

90

drum beats just right and the clarinet-y thing accentuates the right parts. Even the dulcimer dude has got the hang of it. And they're loving it.

Allison herself isn't too keen. She's the image of an oldies-loving mum getting a headache from the ruckus blaring out of her son's room, perched on a now-empty bench. I'm half expecting her to holler at me that I have to turn it down while I'm under her roof else I can start paying her some rent.

Sarah-Jane's having a blast, though. At least I think she is. She's moshing like a good one, with that face that gives the impression that the person's in pain, but they daren't stop and spoil the illusion that they're enjoying themselves. Actually, she wouldn't look out of place at a metal concert – her, or the lords and ladies. Any minute now they'll start a pit.

That doesn't matter, though. This is all for Henry's benefit. I'd nearly forgotten, but as I strum the final chord, it's his eye I try to catch. Only I can't see him. *Shit.* The clapping and cheering and general hubbub is encouraging, gets me buzzing, but I can still feel a weight in my stomach grounding me. Nerves. Talk about a U-turn.

Now, the crowd parts – Bible-style. Henry's storming towards me, and I'm buggered if I can read his expression. I hear the musicians behind me scarper and immediately that stomach-weight doubles. Triples. Quadruples. Would put me through the floor if said floor weren't so bloody *stony*.

'I'm intrigued, Groves,' Henry starts. His voice is low. This can't be good.

'Not your cup of tea?' I try.

I hear Sarah-Jane ask, 'what's *tea*?' and the audible groan as

Allison inevitably elbows her in the ribs. I'm too scared to scoff at her.

'I am intrigued,' Henry tries again, 'as to wherefore you would hide this gift from me?'

Gift. That's good, isn't it? That's *hopeful.*

'Any man who would enter this hall and rouse this grave-dodging lot is worth his salt ten times over. And ten again! You, young Matty Groves, may have my aid in your quest.'

Bloody hell. He's got me buzzing again, and the weight's taken wings and pissed right off.

'I could kiss you, sire.'

'Please refrain. Come, sit down and take your fill. You ladies, too!' He says, grabbing Sarah-Jane and Allison by the shoulders and walking them back to his table.

We squeeze in next to Henry – 'to his *right*!' Allison remarks, so that must be good – and tuck into the spread. I forget any manners and go straight for the meat and roasties.

14
Matty

Once we've stuffed our guts, or "taken our fill" as Sarah-Jane put it, Henry gets emotional. Or dead serious. It's hard to tell because the wine's been flowing.

'I shall be honest, Groves,' Henry starts. Here we go – cue him telling me I'm his best mate, really, no, from the bottom of his heart, really, I am, and chucking up while I order us an Uber home, or a horse as the case would probably be. But he surprises me.

'Donald is more to me than a knave. The very balance of Old England is at stake.'

'Right,' I mutter, rolling my eyes because the last thing I want to get caught up in is political bull. Then I twig.

'Sire, you said *Old* England. Does that mean –?'

He nods.

'You catch me, Groves. I know not how many years have passed in your world – *my* world – but yon Donald is the reason I be here. He and his accursed pawn of a sorcerer.'

I look at Allison, sitting back and picking at her teeth with her wand. I expect her to catch my eye and elaborate, seeing as it's more her territory than mine, but her eyes are locked firmly on Sarah-Jane. Specifically, Sarah-Jane's arse up in the air as she reaches across for the hat of the jester who's just rocked up and is telling her jokes. I'm not going to get any sense out of either of them, so it's up to me to try and talk magic. Bullshitting, as always. At least when I'm with Sandy I tend to get her support.

'So, you really are *the* Henry VIII?'

'I am, I am!' He beams. He's a real piss-taking bastard, even if he doesn't know it. 'His sorcerer, Thackeray, made the passing over. Ask me not how, Groves, I'm no magician. Yet he found his way to my court, and my fools of servants showed him in, if you please! Claimed he could show us magic. I, like a fool, did find myself persuaded to play a part in his marvellous vanishing act. Said it was a sing-song – and from a *book*, if you will! And vanish I did. At least from there. My dear Catherine must ere be ill with worry.'

Despite all he's said, and its relevance, I've just got to ask:

'*Which* Catherine, sire?'

'What mean you, "which Catherine"? My Iberian beauty, by Jove.'

He means Aragon – the first one, then. I can't bring myself to mention the subsequent five. That would just be too much for him to get his head around.

'Wherefore did Thackeray summon thee, then?' Sarah-Jane, despite the silly hat now cocked on her head, appears to have been half-listening at least.

'I presume because this England needed a king, 'pon the death of the previous. No heir, you see.'

'Dear old King John,' Sarah-Jane affirms, crossing her breast.

'But what has any of that got to do with Donald?' I ask.

Henry's face screws up, eyes narrow. He leans into me as though he's about to share some terrible secret with me. I put my face close to his and cop a face full of kingly belch that echoes over the conversations of the other courtiers.

'No idea, lad!' He reaches for another leg of meat.

'Then why do you hate him so much?'

'Ah, you see. Here the malice lies. Despite his sorcerer's pains to bring me here, he has taken it upon himself to challenge my right to reign and enchant the populace of East Kent so that they think him right. *My* populace. Methinks he be a warmonger, plotting away up there in his Leeds Castle.'

That sounds familiar.

'Leeds Castle?'

'Lies beyond the village of Maidstone, lad.' Henry beams. 'Methinks it be there your Sandy doth… take *residence*.'

Well, it's the first lead we've had, and that's something. I can't even bring myself to say, "thank you", I'm feeling that grateful. I want to ask him more about that Thackeray, because something's not quite adding up – why would he bring over another king if his master wants power? Instead, I shiver. It feels like someone's just chucked a bucket of ice water over me, and my arms go goosebump central. Whatever else Henry's said is lost, and he's tucking into a chicken leg. I turn to Allison.

'Is it me, or is it chilly in here?'

It can't be me. The fire's roaring behind me and I've been

sweating for the past hour, but it's better to ask. I daren't *moan* that I'm cold, else Allison will do that mum face telling me it's my own fault for not listening and bringing a jumper. She manages the next best thing.

'I've a cloak, you've no sleeves. Do the arithmetic,' she slurs, putting her hand out for the wine decanter again. 'Though now you mention it, there be a chill in the air.'

She withdraws her hand and looks around her, but nobody else appears to have noticed the cold like we have. They're all still getting on with their grub. I see Allison root around inside her cloak under the table and know she must be going for her wand. Something's up.

I turn to Sarah-Jane, wanting to ask her the same thing and get a half-decent answer, but she's back to sodding about with the jester. I think he's been teaching her how to juggle. He must be failing because there's a potato floating in his bowl and the pair of them are smothered in gravy.

I watch her bat his hand away as he tries to wipe her chest clean when the candle in front of me snuffs. It doesn't blow out, it actually snuffs like an invisible *snuffer* has just done its thing.

I know how these things work. I'm aware of the horror trope I'm being set up for. Any minute there'll be a shadow, or a ghost just casually cross the space I can see out of the corner of my eye. Or else some otherworldly writing will appear on the wall in dubious bodily fluids. Or something will get chucked across the room and somebody'll holler "GHOST!". I'm not taking any chances after the last time – witchy stereotypes? I got a witch. Ghost stereotypes, though – nah, mate, you're all right.

'D'you reckon we should make a move?' I ask the girls.

'I concur, Matty,' Sarah-Jane says, standing to attention and scowling at the jester. 'We must away to your ladylove and not trifle here a moment longer.'

Henry slams his goblet down.

'Friends, must you depart now? We've a hunt tomorrow, you would be most welcome to rest here and join us.'

'Yea, verily, your highness,' Allison says, stifling a burp and wobbling to her feet, 'we must make provision while the day is lit. We thank thee for thy gracious hospitality—'

Suddenly, it's dark. Proper dark like its night, and the big light's just blown in the front room. All candles and torches are snuffed out, like the one in front of me, and there's not even any natural light coming in through the window-holes any more. Everyone in court's beyond pissed.

'What be this sorcery?'

'Ho! Watch where you put that knife!'

'Somebody fetch a torch from the passage!'

It's chaos, but I've known worse when the trains at home aren't running. Someone grabs my wrist and pulls me, like I'm a kid, so I can only assume it's Allison, doing her thing. I'd shake her off, but something stops me. A noise, underneath all the ruckus from the courtiers. It's low and rumbling, and constant, like the thrum of my Traveller's engine when it's actually running sweet. Allison's noticed it too, for she's stopped dead and her grip on me has tightened.

The rumbling carries on, growing louder and louder, silencing the court gradually as they all twig it one by one. It's unbearable.

Something bangs – the doors burst open with pressure, and a wind like icy knives cuts through the hall, shrieking as it blows. Beneath the din, there's another sound – a steady beat, steady as a bass drum. It almost sounds like the thumping of feet, getting nearer and nearer.

Someone behind me moans, as if to say "Christ's *sake*" when next door's crying baby wakes you up in the middle of the night and you've got an early rise the next day. I think it's Henry. I'm about to ask him what the crack is and why he sounds so bloody *knowing* about this supernatural bull when I remember something.

This has happened before. It hits me full in the face, like it must have hit that Greek Eureka bloke. I've *sung* about this poxy story, like I've sung about Allison and Sarah-Jane and goodness knows what else is heading our way because they're all from the bloody English folk songs that Sandy loves so much. Only I can't think about that now because something's walked into the room. And it's a great big –

'GHOST!'

She's not a horrible ghost, except for the fact she's glowing white. For some reason, it gives everything else in the room a purple tinge. Oh, and she's about twenty feet tall, as high as the hall. *"Her head hit the roof-tree of the house, her middle you could not span."* Well, that last bit's not exactly true. She's *hot*. In the ethereal sense. Each step she takes shakes the room, and she nearly toes some of the lords and ladies in the head as they run for their lives.

'Some meat!' She hollers. It's probably her normal speaking

voice, but it echoes in a way that it sounds like a shout. It still makes me nervous though, and her breath is like a breeze of its own.

'She'll not rest until she's taken her fill – you were better make haste,' Henry instructs.

'Aye, but will *you* be all right?' Sarah-Jane hollers into the wind.

Henry scoffs, his wind-tears streaming.

'My dear, a meddlesome ghost is naught by comparison to a foreign wife! Knowest thou that we speak in Latin to one another?'

Part of me wants to stay and help the poor sod. The rest of me is grateful we've got his blessing to hop it. Allison holds her wand straight up, and something see-through shoots up, and forms something like an umbrella. It's sort of invisible, and I can almost feel heat waves. It covers the three of us. I'm guessing this is some weird stealth tactic, and I wonder why she couldn't have used this when we turned up at the castle. Oh, there are plenty of bones I want to pick with the woman.

We sneak out the way we came, following the crowd and taking a few of them out with our invisibility cocoon, leaving Henry at the ghost's mercy. Though I've a funny feeling, he'll be okay.

15

Sandy

My back's killing as I crouch down and make my way along the perimeter of the house. I've got to be invisible. Were I at home, I'd have probably gone to my room with the hump and cranked up the record player to piss my parents off. But I can't do that here, not least because of ageing weirdoes that might sneak up on me.

But I've got to meet Ellyn and see these farmhands. Just show my face in case his lordship asks her about me, but as soon as they get down to their sexy business I'm away on one of his horses. It's simple, and Christ knows if it'll work, but I've got to try. Anything to get away from the House of a Thousand Mental Cases.

The ground dips and I nearly go headfirst into a pig's trough, guts in my chest and heart on overdrive. I think I might have stepped in something too, which is just bloody great, and I can't see bugger all to try and wipe my foot.

The stables are around the corner, and I'm glad when I see the silhouettes of Ellyn and a couple of other girls, just picked out by a solitary torch that one of them is holding.

'All right, girls?' I ask, rubbing my hands together because it's a bit nippy tonight, even for May.

'We thought something had befallen you, my la– *Sandy*,' Ellyn says, hugging me. I wish she wouldn't. She stinks worse than the crap on my foot. The first thing I'm doing when I get back is having a bath.

'Ought we to depart, then?' One of the girls says.

'This is Abigail, and that's Mercy,' Ellyn explains. Both girls nod and wave when they hear their respective names, and we start off towards the cow fields. Abigail, I notice, has a limp which I'd imagine to be gout or else some other ailment that's easily cured with the meds back home. Mercy won't stop talking, and every time something comes out of her mouth she scratches under her cloth cap. I won't be getting too close to her – I don't need an action replay of the nit treatment circa last year of junior school.

'Is it far, where we're meeting these guys?' I ask, trying to hide my hope that it's as far from Donald's place as possible.

'Trouble yourself not, Sandy,' Ellyn says, swinging her torch high so that all I want to do is trouble myself. 'At the end of this field – you'll not see it just now, but there's a brook. We follow it ten minutes hence, and the boys will be at the mouth of the wood.'

So, it's a quick shag in the bushes, then. Things really don't change. I'm excited by the prospect of woods, though – where *there are* woods, there's a chance of getting lost. Not the best scenario normally, but it's exactly what I need now. I only wish I had the dog with me. The other Matty Groves. The *real* Matty Groves. I can still hardly believe that this place is just one massive folk song. And not just any – a staple that everyone and their mothers had a pop at. At least my Matty's not here to endure it. I'd quite like to explore if I knew what was what and wasn't just a prisoner.

We continue in silence, treading slowly alongside a brook that's making me want to have a wee because of the noise. Sure enough, there's a dark mass beneath the purple sky that looks a lot like trees.

Five minutes later, I can see those farmhands in the half-light. They're illuminated by their own torch and waving madly to the girls who have picked up the pace. It's sweet to feel their excitement, hear their hurried steps and heavier breaths. It makes me wish that Matty really was coming for me, like I'd told crackpots one and two.

Ellyn launches herself into the arms of her boy, burying her head in his neck – and that, for some bloody bizarre reason, really strikes it home. And hard. Matty's got this certain way of cuddling me, one arm around my shoulders, and the other in my hair that he's asked me so many times to cut because he thinks it'll look "cute" on me, but I know it's because he's got a thing for super short hair on girls. I've seen what's on his laptop. But he still loves playing with the hair I've got, nuzzling into my ear. And it fills me up with joy until I overflow, joy I can see on Ellyn's face now. He might get on my wick sometimes, but *Christ*, I miss Matty.

My eyes start to prickle, but I can't cry. I daren't cry, not while everyone's so happy. A whack on the shoulder brings me back to the world of the living.

'Yea, Sandy, what say you?'

Crap, I think I was meant to be listening. I'll do what I normally do and just agree and worry about it later.

'I say… whatever you say, Ellyn.'

Everyone cracks up at that, so it evidently wasn't the right answer.

'I say that life is brief and that if you be offered the chance to cavort, then you would be a fool to pursue it not.'

'Cavort?' There's a word.

The guy with Mercy spits and turns to me, his hand still on Mercy's tit.

'Aye, my brother is equipped well and will treat you kind, lady. If you will only stay a while, I can fetch him ten minutes hence.'

No fear. I've got a horrible feeling that I know what's up.

'That's really… considerate of you and that, but I'll be all right, ta.'

Ellyn frowns.

'Sandy, your spirits seemed risen when I extended the invitation to join us. Do we now do you an embarrassment?'

Now I'm well lost. The last thing I'm feeling is embarrassed, but her face has gone white.

'You'll not tell Donald of our mischief, Sandy?' She pulls at my hoodie. 'Oh, I could not stand that! Please, Sandy – my lady!'

Ellyn is nearly throttling me with material now and sobbing into my chest. I wonder if it's her tears or actually her that smells of onions.

'Whoa, Ellyn – I'm not going to tell on you. Not a word. You've been so good to me, inviting me out and that. You've been the closest thing to a friend I've had since coming here. But I would ask you one thing.'

'Oh, anything, Sandy!'

'Well, Matty – that's my boyfriend–'

'A male friend?'

Shit, what's the word?

'Well, companion – *lover,* what have you. I've got to find him. We got split up, when I came here. I'll go to him, alone – through the woods – but you mustn't tell Donald. Is that all right?'

Ellyn nods, wiping her nose on her sleeve. The trail of snot glimmers in the torchlight and makes me want to vom.

'Of course, my la– *Sandy.'*

'I need to go now if I want to be out of here by the morning – please, d'you mind if I take one of the torches?'

She shrinks, and I don't know why. Until somebody behind me speaks.

'I would mind. The lady will not venture further.'

Bugger that stupid condescending old bastard voice. I turn around. It's Thacks. And he's got the dog, holding him by the scruff of his neck.

'I bloody will,' I say, not taking my eyes off the dog. 'Give him to me, I'm taking him away from all you loonies and I'm going to see Matty.'

'Think of what you say, Sandy,' he says, twisting the dog's scruff. The poor thing starts to lick its lips and tries to jerk free, but he only tightens his grip. 'True, I may not do anything to you under my lord's watch. But he be not here. I may do all that I desire short of killing you.'

'You wouldn't dare! What are you gonna do, hit me? Bruise me? Or worse? Donald will kill you and you know it.'

He seems to tighten his grip on the dog even more then. Everyone's run off. Some friends. They're all gone, except for Ellyn who looks like her eyes are going to pop right out of her head.

'Sandy, prithee not goad him so!'

'Perhaps so,' says Thacks. 'But then think you on your canine friend.'

As if to make a point, he tries lifting him up by the scruff, but the good old boy manages to twist out of his grip and run to me.

'I'll kill you myself if you ever touch this dog!'

'Oh? We shall see!'

I can't read his expression. I don't have to. He claps his hands together twice, murmuring something, and an awful red electricity shoots straight out of his hands as he thrusts them out. It surrounds the dog as he's ripped from my hands and floats in mid-air like an electric halo. We all stare at him for a moment in shock, before his front legs are yanked by an invisible force which makes him yelp. They're pulled out parallel to the ground, and he hangs there like a doggy Christ, his head snapping side to side as though an invisible hand is slapping him.

'Stop it, you monster!' I hear my voice crack, but I don't care. Thacks only laughs as I try to grab him. He forces me to the ground with one hand.

'Think your tears are enough to stop this creature's pain? You must take greater pains yet!'

Right. There's a pile of logs underneath one of the trees, like somebody's been cutting firewood and forgotten to take it with them. I run to it, grabbing the biggest one I can, and try to strike Thacks with it. I never make contact. He uses one hand to hold the dog in position, and the other he points at me.

I've never known pain like it. I drop the log immediately and as I'm lifted into the air, it feels like wasps are stinging every vein and artery in my body. It's constant, up and down my arms and legs and inside my head and my chest and everywhere else, all at the same time. I can't help but cry as I see the dog floating across from me, panting in full distress, all cried out, and it's too much.

'My lady!' Ellyn is crying herself, now. 'Master, please stop this. I shall inform my lord of your crime!'

'And what?' He sneers. 'Who shall he believe – the word of his oldest and most trusted friend, or that of lowly kitchen scum like you? One word to my lord, and you shall never work in service again.'

Everything's going white, and I can only hear the panting and the crying over the tinnitus in my ears. I can just about see Ellyn hunched over on her knees, and I know that there's more at stake than just me and the dog.

'Leave it, Ellyn,' I say, though I'm not sure if she can hear me. 'Please, Thackeray, I'll do whatever you want. Honest. Do what you want to me. Just leave the dog and Ellyn alone.'

'Very well. Perhaps now you will know your place.'

16
Matty

'I can't believe it,' I say, once we're finally settled and we've got a fire going.

Sarah-Jane grinds her knuckles into my head and grins.

'Fear not. The talk of war is only –'

'I mean, Henry VIII has been here? *Alive*? All these centuries? What does that say about time, here? And at home? What about the Henry VIII history tells us about? Replaced? Conspiracy? And then there's that sodding *ghost* and the fact that you should all be fictional, but you're actually *real*.'

Allison hands me a knife.

'If you're to ramble, you can at least be productive while you do it. Peel the potatoes for me.'

'What potatoes?'

She whispers something into her sleeve, pokes her wand up there like she's digging around until three potatoes come tumbling out indignantly to the ground.

'You ought to start charging for that. You'd make a fortune,' I say, wiping the nearest one on my jeans.

It's like a proper little campsite here. Once we hotfooted it out of the castle, away from the ghost palaver, we made for the woods about two miles inland. This all would have been way easier if they only had cars here, because I'd have known the bloody way to Donald's castle. But of course, they don't, and we're back to bare basics. And that's people telling you it's in the general direction they're pointing, and did you want to buy a horse to carry you there, and if you did that would be fifteen gold coins and your trainers, or "queer foot trappings". Sarah-Jane had words with the bloke that had asked for those, and we had to drag her away before she "blacked his eyes for him and worse." At least she's getting to let out a bit of whatever's pent up in her now. As I peel, chucking the potato skins and cradling the veg with my crossed legs, I watch her. She's stalking something between two trees, just outside our mini clearing, bent low and sword poised. How she'll catch any grub with that I'll never know. But then they all seem to know so much more than me, and I hate it.

'Fie!' Sarah-Jane hollers. Up I leap, potatoes everywhere. Where's her *chill*?

'Missed it?' Allison asks, dusting the potatoes on her sleeve and dropping them into a big metal pot. I won't even ask where she managed to get that from.

'Aye. But hold!' She holds a finger up. Takes a step, and…
schunk.

'Ho! Would you but *look* at this one?'

I look. I wish I hadn't. On her sword, speared right through, is a huge brown rabbit, flopped over. And guts. And who knows what else?

'Well done, Sarah-Jane! Oh, what a feast we shall have!'

Allison claps her hands.

'Wait, we're gonna *eat* that?' My guts are rumbling, and I'm deadbeat after all the walking. The banquet from earlier has been well and truly worked off. But I can't bear the thought of it. I know people eat rabbit, but he's still got all his fur and his head and that.

As if reading my mind, Sarah-Jane fetches him over.

'Would you skin it, Matty?'

***

In the end, Allison skinned it. I'd covered my eyes for that bit, even though she did it all with the wand. I hate to admit it but cooking on the fire next to the potatoes it smells *munch*.

It's all a bit cosy, what with the cooking smell and the sun just peeking through and giving its last little bit of light, ready for the night. It should be cold, but Allison's poked her wand in the ground, point up. Just like the umbrella earlier on, it's producing another dome, but bigger – a *tent*, around forty feet in diameter. You can just see the reflections of the flames in the membrane, yet it's entirely see-through and – so Allison says – impermeable. I think that means nothing can get in or out.

Sarah-Jane's just testing that out at the minute. She's prodded it with a finger, punched it, and now she's getting ready to take a run up and ram the bastard.

'I would refrain from that, were I you,' Allison says, sprawling on a patch of heather. It's said in that way that's reproachful but hinting that they really want to see you try because you're doomed to fail, and they could do with a good laugh. Sarah-Jane goes for it regardless, running the entire diameter. She heads shoulder-first into the membrane, and there's a loud smack as she makes contact before reeling backwards. She lands arse-first.

'Are you okay?' I jump up from my stump to give her a hand up.

'Aye, well – it's her own fault, be she injured.' Allison sniffs.

I pull Sarah-Jane to her feet, and she shakes herself like a dog that's winded itself through playing too much. Then she grins.

'Allison's right – there's nothing can get through that!'

She spits, and plops herself down next to Allison, sticking a hand into the fire and helping herself to a bit of bunny. She blows on it, then swallows the chunk whole. I've *got* to tell her.

'There's a word for women like you, where I come from,' I say, poking the fire with a stick. 'Ever heard of a "badass"?'

She sits up defensively.

'Matty, think you bad of me?'

'Nah – "badass" means good. You're *cool*.'

Allison sniggers.

'The lad's off his head. It's warm as a summer's day in here.'

'You don't get it. Cool is good – awesome. Like the way you just don't give a shit about what people think. And you took on all them men, with swords, and didn't even break a sweat.'

She spits again, unknowingly illustrating my point.

'Experience, Matty – I've *lived*.'

I nod as it clicks, and I can't help but feel a bit jealous.

'You're in a song, too,' I say, thinking back on it. 'That's what's happening here. Is it true – did you kill William's mistress? And did your captain really make you a commander?'

Allison props herself up on her elbows, apparently eager to hear. Sarah-Jane laughs in her throat, and her eyes are glazed in the firelight.

'Captain Hardy was a good man. He did extend the offer to me. Methinks I did impress him with the deed – yes, I shot the other Lady Taylor. I was aiming for William.'

She meets Allison's look and they both crack up like a pair of old hags. Well, I guess it's almost appropriate for at least one of them.

'Seems Hardy thought I shot the lady for honour's sake. I suppose it was all for that, at first. Hardy did seek to promote me, to be a commander in His Majesty's Navy. But I declined. I felt I had to bring William to justice – for bedding another, while I had resigned to wait for him, as a good wife should. Indeed, we were bound for his trial when you came by us.' She smiles at me and pulls idly at the heather by her hip. 'But even if I *did* want to command, it wouldn't be allowed. Women aren't even allowed to *board* some ships here, let alone command them.'

'Well, that's a load of bollocks. You'd have the *tumblr* crew up in arms,' I say, shuddering. You know better than to get on the wrong side of them when the Social Justice Warriors at college have got you up against the lockers outside the Art room. It's even worse when your girlfriend has to rescue you because she's mates with them.

'Aye, well the crew of His Majesty's *Tumblar* know not this land. *This*,' she says, pulling at her shirt, 'this disguise is the only way I could gain passage in the first place. And I'll be condemned to the fires of Hell if I would go back in a maiden's weeds. This feels... *right*, somehow.' She smiles and rubs her knees. 'Still, the *fuss* when my mother caught me cutting off my hair. You'd have thought I'd lost a limb!'

'Oh, but your hair is *lovely*,' Allison says, colouring slightly. Almost outing herself. She basically does, now, as she reaches for an errant lock to push back from Sarah-Jane's face. It's too cute, and I can't stop myself from saying it.

'For God's sake. Just *kiss* her, will you?'

'Pardon?'

'Matty!' Allison retracts her hand like Sarah-Jane's a nettle, and she's just been stung. Her eyes are wide and her mouth is open like a fish, as if I've just said the most amazing thing in the world.

'Look, if this was a book or a film or something, and you were being observed, imagined, then you'd have a fan base – admirers. And they would ship the shit out of you two.'

'What is it with your people and *boats*?'

'No, your *ship*,' I correct Sarah-Jane. 'People love a bit of tension.'

'Ah,' she says, even though she doesn't seem to have a clue. 'And what is a *film*?'

I don't even want to try explaining that one. I just smile at her and shrug.

'Something from my world. Perhaps I can show you, one day.'

I wish I hadn't said anything at all, now, as we tuck into our rabbit and potatoes. The girls' eyes are clamped firmly on the food on their knees, or the fire. It's even more awkward than when the gym wankers helped themselves to my rucksack and found my lyric book. It would have been okay had it been a Beatles compendium or something. But these lyrics were *mine*, my own pretentious scribbles passing for rock songs in a scruffy little spiral-bound notebook with a skull on the front. I guess it was almost my own modern version of the book we'd found in the pub, the one that caused all this. I'd hoped to show my lyrics to Sandy one day, when they were ready, and had visions of her throwing her arms around me and saying yes, why couldn't we do some rock songs as well, because you're a talented lyricist, Matty, a real Bob Dylan or Alex Turner. Well, she got to see them. Everyone at college got the opportunity, once the gym lot had photocopied pages in the library and left them all over the grounds.

I flick a rabbit bone in the fire. The bastards saw it all, everything that I'd kept bottled up over the past two years and could only let out on paper or in song. Private stuff. Stuff about Sandy, stuff about my parents' divorce. Even stuff about my fear of not making it to uni, or worse, making it to uni and doing well but still ending up on the dole. Worst of all was a work-in-progress that I'd titled *Shaven Sheila*, about my "penchant for obscenely short hair on girls" as Sandy had once put it. The premature outing really didn't help my reputation as a weirdo. But Sandy hadn't cared, she'd thought it was sweet. She respected it. And she was the one to tell the gym lot to do one, because at least I had an interest in something other than flexing in a mirror like a bunch of wankers. A tutor was behind her when she said that, creasing up, but we still got sent to "talk it out" with the on-site counsellor. Come to think of it, Sandy had rescued me then, too. Just like she always has. Suddenly, I'm not so hungry. I dump the rest of my dinner in the embers.

'Sarah-Jane, can I ask you something?'

She does that annoying thing of answering my question with a question, spitting a mouthful of potato at me with it.

'Are you *crying*?'

'What? No.' I put my hand to an eye, and it's moist. 'No, bollocks am I. It's the smoke, the fire.'

"Twould be a brave thing to admit your fear, Matty,' Allison says. She offers me a scrap of cloth from somewhere in her cloak. 'I know you have had not the chance to process everything entirely.'

'I don't want your smelly tissue. I'm not crying.'

Allison stiffens and crosses her arms.

'Then what *do* you want?' Sarah-Jane says.

She's still got both our swords, tucked away behind the stump I'm sitting on. I bring the one she gave me out, and her eyes light up.

'I know I'm... a bit bad at all of this.'

Allison has what looks like a minor seizure laughing.

'But it's not my fault! We don't have swordfights where I'm from. We've moved on. If we want to settle something, we do it with fists.' *Even if I can't*, I don't add.

'Sounds to me as though your world has regressed.'

'Whatever. Maybe, actually. But I'm sick of everyone always taking the rise out of me. I want to be able to do things for myself and not keep having to be rescued by a bloody witch or by someone who's braver than I'll ever be.'

There's a pause. Allison nudges Sarah-Jane.

'He means *us*, wise one.'

'Ah!'

I sit on the floor in front of Sarah-Jane and hold the sword out to her like I'm making a ritual offering. In spite of the fire, in spite of our cosy bubble, I'm shaking. This is way more intense than any stage fright.

'Look, I know you've helped me so much already, and it's really nice and everything, and I know I don't deserve it after how I treated Sandy, and, I dunno. With you both being here, it makes me feel like I'm not such a dipshit after all. But Sand could die, and I want to do just one half decent thing in my poxy life and save her. So, would you please, *please* show me how to shit some people up with this?'

***

It's impossible to become Errol Flynn in one night, but you can certainly learn how to defend yourself, even if your form isn't quite right and your blows are sloppy. I guess we'll get to the shitting people up part later. Sarah-Jane seemed pleased to have been picked for a tutor, because she never stopped smiling, not even when I nearly took her arm off. We practiced all night, well past the time you try sneaking into the club without ID. Or so I'm guessing, seeing as we've not got a watch between us.

She taught me to block my opponent – that's the most important one– and a few basic moves that will inflict a bit of damage.

'And if all else fails, whether you are cornered or unable to counter him, you may kick him where it hurts,' she said.

'You want me to do him in the nuts? That's low, that's a *girl's* move,' I said.

'Aye, and so too is biting. Yet I saw you do the very same to the king's guard. Just you think on that,' she said, and Allison had cackled long and hard thinking back on our scuffle. 'I speak truth Matty – how you do it matters not, only defend yourself.'

It's easier said than done. I'm aching even now as I lay here, sunlight warming my face as I wake myself up. I peer over my chest.

This morning, something's not right. Allison and Sarah-Jane are still asleep, even though it's light. That's not it, even though you'd expect Ye Olde Englanders to be up at the crack of dawn. I reach behind me and prod the gelatine wall. The dome is still up and functioning, so everything's all right there.

I sit up and look about. The fire's still there, smouldering. The clearing's just as it was. Everything's quiet. Silent, in fact. That's what it is – no birdsong. Not that that's a bad thing when you're trying to get your full seven or eight hours.

Christ knows what time it is. I don't want to wake the girls up just yet, though. They're spooning and look all cosy and sweet. Sarah-Jane's got her thumb in her mouth and I really wish I had my phone, so I could take a photo and rib her with it. Guess I'll practice some of the moves she taught me last night, while she's unable to take the piss out of me. Thinking about it, I'd best go for a pee myself.

I stretch and flip onto all fours. The heather bed wasn't bad,

116

but it's nowhere near as soft as folksong makes out. Combined with last night's workout, I've killed my back. I get up slowly, staring at the bush the other side of the dome. Funny, I don't remember it being there when I fell asleep. I'd have wanted to kip somewhere away from bugs, impermeable walls or not.

'Weird,' I mutter. I make sure my back's to the girls and go to unzip my jeans. The bush bristles.

No. I'm still sleepy. It's just the wind. Bushes don't bristle. They also don't have eyes, like this one does.

'Allison!'

It didn't feel like any sound came out, but all at once Allison's beside me, hair even wilder than usual and flowers imprinted in her cheek.

'What?'

She won't be able to use her wand. It's holding up the only thing between us and it. But she might be able to shoo it. I grab my sword and use it to point.

'There's someone in that bush.'

She squints at the bush, immobile. Piss-taking.

'You are mistaken. 'Tis but a philadelphus. Rather good for enemies, if you stew the flowers long enough.'

'No, it had *eyes*. There were eyes, looking right at me.'

She sighs and rubs the dribble crust from her face.

'I'll awaken Sarah-Jane.'

I don't turn to watch her. I'm focused on the bush. There are no eyes now. But it moved and looked at me, I'm sure of it. I think I've been here long enough to accept that mad things that shouldn't ever happen are the norm.

Sarah-Jane yawns beside me.

117

'You look like a pointing dog, Matty. Be sure your eyes exit your skull not.'

'Hilarious.'

'The boy believes the bush did move,' Allison says. 'And had eyes that met his.'

'Well, he's not wrong, is he? *Look.*'

One point to me in the not losing your marbles competition. The bush trembles, then shakes. Violently. The shaking is so strong that the membrane of the dome quakes where it touches, and pops like a bubble. We take a collective walk backwards.

The shaking halts. Birds shoot out of the trees, all around us, and the sky above us explodes into colours and noise. Under our feet, there's a rumble. Hundreds of squirrels, rabbits, badgers, in fact the whole bloody cast of *The Animals of Farthing Wood* come out from the trees and sprint towards us. Past us. Allison runs and snatches up her wand before the critters get there and twirls it in her hand like a magical majorette.

Sarah-Jane palms her sword. We watch mushrooms and flowers of all colours erupt in the wake of the running animals, making two lines – a *path* – straight to us.

'You remember what we practiced?' Sarah-Jane mouths at me.

I nod, lifting my own sword, but I can't concentrate. The animals line up, forming actual little ranks, either side of the path. The bush at the end trembles again, and then rolls. It lifts itself up on branchy legs and rolls – *tumbles* – towards us, down the path. The animals begin to chitter and squeal in delighted wild animal chorus. It's a real forest circus. I just hope we're not the clowns.

17
Sandy

It wasn't Ellyn's fault at all, though you'd think it had been going by the way she cried. I can still see her face all twisted up and ugly even after he let us down, ingrained in my head and the walls of the room they've locked me in. This one doesn't have any of the finery that was in my previous room. But at least I've got the dog this time, and he's okay despite his ordeal. I must stop calling him that. Matty Dog, his name will be. Any minute I might burst into song and start talking with him like an animated, hard-done-by maiden that's not become a princess yet. And no way am I about to marry beardy old weirdies. I've seen the films, read the books, sung the songs – the creeps always tend to get their way. But not this time.

Matty Dog nuzzles further into my lap, as though he can hear my thinking out loud. Poor guy gets it – if he really is *the* Matty Groves, not dead as in the story, but transmogrified, then he gets it more than anyone.

'So, *Matty*,' I start. Christ, it's weird calling him that. 'How was it?'

He lifts his head slightly to look at me – it still throws me how he understands everything I have to say. He just stares, until I realise I didn't explain what it was.

'When you… did the business with Lady Donald. Did you love her?'

He wags his tail then and licks my hand. That's got to be a definite doggy "yes".

'I'm sorry. I'm sorry for your loss – and Donald's. I'm sorry they did this to you.' I scratch behind his ears, and he settles again. 'When we get out of here – if we get out – you can come home with me. Honest. Though I don't know how I'll explain you to my Mum. I don't know how I'll explain any of this, or if I even should. They must be going potty back home.'

Home. I can't help it. The word sticks in my throat, and I can feel that weird sting behind my eyes. There's no stopping it. I twist over, burying my face in Matty Dog's neck, and sob.

It's a while before I hear the door to the chamber open – a loud *clunk* of unlocking, the groan of the wood – but I don't look up. I won't let anyone see me with a wet face, weak. Especially not Thackeray. He can sod right off.

'That was some courage you found, girl.'

It's not Thackeray's voice. I look up immediately, wiping my cheeks with the sleeve of my hoodie. It's Donald himself.

'No henchman today?' I manage. I cough immediately afterwards like some twat. I wish I had my asthma pump. Donald doesn't seem to notice.

'Alas, no. Would happen that the old fool is insufferable to me presently.' He lingers by the door, as though trying to decide whether he wants to come in.

'Bollocks. You don't do anything without him.'

'He is… necessary. Truth be known, I would dispense with him, if not for you.'

That seems to make up his mind. He closes the door behind him and sits on the floor next to me. I shuffle as far away from him as I can without disturbing Matty Dog.

'What d'you mean, "dispense with him"?'

He doesn't answer me immediately, just makes shapes with his mouth and runs his finger down the cracks between the stones on the floor, where there'd be some half-decent grouting in civilised society. Calculating the safest thing to say to me, I'll bet.

'Thackeray is a puzzle.'

Matty Dog lifts his head and narrows his doggy eyes at Donald.

'I mean it. He is an insufferable fool, yet without him I am nothing.'

I tuck my knees up under my chin. Despite what he is, the old prat's got me interested in his story. He carries on staring at the stones.

'Please tell him not that I reveal this to you.'

'You think I'm gonna tell that knobend anything? You must be more cracked than I thought.'

He finally looks at me, and his mouth twitches.

'Yes, I suppose I must be. Even now, troops mobilise beneath Donald's banner, ready to march against King Henry and I've given never an order for it. The king may curse me, but his hatred was better targeted at Thackeray.'

I don't understand what he's on about, but I think I get the gist.

'Donald is that bearded old twit *blackmailing* you?'

Silence.

'He is, isn't he? He wants to take over and needs you to do it. Christ, why can't you man up and do something about it? You're a lord, aren't you?'

'Sandy, a title is only that. Thackeray has the real power. He's the only one who can bring my Benevolence home to me.'

I sigh. It's breaking my heart, I know what the soppy old sod's going through, but it's also my life on the line.

'Donald, you don't marry and kill people to bring someone else back. It sounds stupid, but where I come from, if somebody dies, you do move on eventually. And you honour their memory, so they never really die.'

'Sorcery indeed,' he says. He shifts from one arse cheek to the other. 'You make me a villain, Sandy. Yet I keep you in luxury. I offer you a seat at my table, the finest food. I house you in the grandest building. You've your own chamber, your every whim catered for, and I would clothe you in the most wondrous weeds would you only allow it.'

'Yeah, about that. Your style is a *lot* to be desired.'

'Then I shall distribute your dresses among the ladies of the household. You need not don such vestments while here. What of that?'

I look at Matty Dog, who's fallen asleep again, and don't look Donald in the eye. I daren't.

'I'd say that's pretty all right of you.'

The chamber door thunders open and cuts our therapy session short. In storms Thacks, his face is the colour of his beard and wringing his hands.

Donald stands and brushes the dust from his cloak.

'What ails you, Thackeray?'

'I have been in conference with the spirits of the ball. The boy is on his way.'

Matty. It's got to be him. The stupid idiot, what's his game? I leap to my feet, my head spinning. My ears ring, and I want to be sick. He's actually here, somewhere.

As if reading my mind, Donald's tone changes.

'Where is he now?'

'I know not. The spirits did show me a wood. He's a cursed witch and a swordsman in tow.'

'What do you advise we do?'

Thacks looks over Donald's shoulder, directly at me.

'Return to your own chamber, wench. This concerns you not.'

But it does. It so bloody does, and I want to gather that beard in my hands and pull until he tells me what the deal is. But I daren't, for Matty Dog's sake. For my sake. I don't want to get electrocuted again. I turn to Matty Dog now.

'Come, boy. Let's leave these men alone.'

I wince even saying it because screw them. But it's on, and I've got to play along with them just long enough. Matty's on his way, and if Thacks is the conniving prick I think he is, it's not going to be an easy ride.

18
Matty

The bush rolls to a stop about three feet in front of us. The animal chorus gets louder, shriller, and hurts my ears. I try to retract my head into my shoulders to cover them, because no way am I letting go of my sword.

A mess of vines shoots from the left side, then another from the right. They plant themselves on the ground, forming bent arms. The fingers, or collection of twigs, on both ends seemingly rearrange themselves and drum as though thinking.

Then, a voice from within the bush speaks.

'You were better stood back, mortals.'

It gives us no time to shift, though, as it lifts itself up on the two arms. A branchy foot kicks free of the bush, missing my head by inches. Another grazes Allison's cloak. It stands, the legs extending the thing to its full height, which must be about eight feet tall. It would be almost humanoid, only it's missing a head. The animals fall silent as the bush man rustles all over. That's the sound of even more leaves unfurling all over it and covering its brown bits until finally it resembles a wilder version of a topiary statue. Finally, its head extends out from its chest, as though it had been snapped at the neck, and rises to the top. Its hair falls down over its shoulders in leafy abundance, and its eyes – the *same* eyes – open. Its beard jiggles from side to side as though its non-existent nose has a twitch.

I can barely believe it. I've seen the face before.

'You're the bastard on the front of the book!'

Its eyebrows twist up.

'I beg your pardon, young sir?'

'You might just be the cause of all this – a man made of leaves, acorns, and general tree-ness, you're–'

'Ho, now!' His arm grips my shoulder a bit too firm for comfort. 'Son, you have just described the Green Man. Complete figment of the peasantry imagination. I am Jack-in-the-Green – there *is* a difference, you know.'

Allison whispers something to Sarah-Jane, who immediately sheaths her sword.

'Show some respect, will you, Matty? Ordinarily, the Jack exposes himself not to everyday folk like us,' Allison says.

Jack's grip on me loosens, and he takes Allison's now tiny-looking hand in his.

'And ordinarily, the Jack finds himself not in the presence of such a *kind* witch.' He raises it up and bends to kiss it – or rather, brush it with his leaf moustache.

'Aye, so what be the occasion?' Sarah-Jane snaps, eyeing up the gesture.

'Yeah, what's the deal?'

He drops Allison's hand, and stretches his arms over his head, reaching back. I'm half expecting him to say he doesn't know. He's got a face on him looking like one of these kiddies that's done wrong but still claims innocence. But there's a rustle as he digs around in what must be his back, looking for something, and then a snap. He brings his arms back to the front and holds something out to us in his hands.

'Look upon it with your own eyes,' he whispers.

We look.

'Mate, that's just *leaves*.'

And it is. He's just picked off a twelve-inch bit of himself and put it in front of us. Sarah-Jane clamps a hand on me.

'Nay. Look again, Matty.'

So, I look, and I don't get it at first. It's just a bunch of brown leaves, curling at the edges, and crumbling flowers. But then, the rest of him is green. If Jack's a living thing…

'You're dying?' Allison voices what we're all thinking.

The animal audience erupts in what sounds like laughter. Even Jack himself catches the giggles.

'Me, die?' He chuckles, before breaking into a coughing fit. I almost want to pat him on the back, only I wouldn't want to put my hand through him. 'The spirit of nature can never die, not entirely. But I fear I am rather ill. You see, I was awakened some days ago by my creatures, and they did seem perturbed by something. 'Twould appear the balance of nature has been… well, *un*balanced. The animals can sense these things, you know. And they were correct.'

'Aye, well, that'll be the fault of Matty, here,' Allison says, patting me. 'I must apologise on his behalf, Jack.'

'Oi, I've got a mouth!' I turn to Jack. 'Look, I am really sorry for upsetting the balance or what have you. I didn't want to make anyone ill or that.'

'Think naught of it. 'Tis forgotten, as of this branch!' With that, he snaps his twelve-incher in half and tosses it into his animal crowd. 'I have been following you this past day.'

'Because that's not creepy at all, is it?'

'I observed your lesson with this fine girl. It did seem you were preparing to face some foe. I hope you will tell me your purpose, that I may help your journey make haste and restore the balance before too many leaves turn. Before the cold comes and forces my creatures to take leave of this earth. My guardianship extends not far in premature winters.'

It feels like I've been doing a bit too much explaining to folk, real and fictitious. But we go through the rigmarole again – Sandy, book, Allison, Sarah-Jane, Henry. It almost sounds like a cast list. Turns out that Jack had followed us since we fled the castle, and wanted to "observe" us some more, to make sure his animals weren't making stuff up about what they could sense.

'They do that, you know. Oftentimes, it happens that they merely want attention. I doubted them not this time, of course, for I too felt the rip.'

'There!' Allison exclaims. 'It appears you made quite a hole when you passed through the fabric, Matty.'

'Not quite, my dear,' Jack says. A squirrel winds its way up to his shoulder, and he lifts a finger for it to nibble on. 'Two passed through, did they not? Perchance there are two holes.'

'That would explain why Sandy wasn't in the same place I dropped,' I say. 'But what's the relevance?'

'Two tears in the fabric twixt the worlds will allow the coming of the premature winter twice as quickly. I do believe it be in the interests of all to find your ladylove sooner rather than later.' Jack says this last bit in a whisper. The squirrel's gone to sleep in the gap above where his collarbone would be. 'Only the person who passed through can also mend the tear. If she is in mortal danger, we shall need to move fast.'

That'll do me. 'Can you show us a quicker way to Lord Donald, then?'

Jack sets the squirrel down with its squirrelly pals.

'I know not this Donald. But I know a man who does.'

Great, another bloody character. I wonder how I can keep up with them all, this place is like a *who's who* of English folksong. And as for Sandy knowing all their tales and their variations by heart – well, it's impressive. I can't wait to tell her that when I see her again. If I see her again. For some reason, thinking that I might not see her again makes my throat ball up. I'm grateful when Jack continues and saves me from asking.

'Long Lankin is a bit of a hermit these days, but with some persuasion I've never a doubt he will take you to Donald. Methinks they have some… *history* between them.'

But the warning bell went off before that little detail. I remember the tale of Long Lankin, because it was one of Sandy's silly songs that I actually didn't mind. The Lankin in *that* tale was a murderer. Just as Allison is the real *Allison Gross*, with her would-be turning-people-into-worms ways, and Sarah-Jane played her part in *Bold William Taylor*. Just as there really is a ghost in the castle of *King Henry*. And this Jack, who's beckoning us to follow him deeper into the wood, is going to take us straight to the killer of baby, lady, and nurse. A *serial* killer.

Long Lankin.

I grip my sword with both hands and follow the living bush and the girls down a dirt path between the trees. The animals scarper.

Goody.

19
Matty

Long Lankin's cottage in the woods is straight out of another fairy tale, and this time it's an even creepier one than Allison's tower was. The journey wasn't even that long – perhaps fifteen minutes tops, and I really wasn't ecstatic to have spent the night virtually on the murderer's doorstep. I didn't even see the cottage at first – it looked like Jack led us straight to a wooded bank, even more wild and leafy than the bush man himself. Only as we get nearer, I notice a plume of smoke creeping up from the top of the bank, between the trees. A few more steps reveal windows peeking out between patches of growth, and a door of sorts, which is embedded in the dirt at an angle, picked out by various shrubs.

'What manner of man lives as an animal in the ground?' Sarah-Jane says. It's thinking out loud because the last bit's mumbled as though she's twigged her mistake and thought it might be a bit rude. Jack doesn't seem to notice.

'Take care with your foot-falls,' he says, choosing his steps carefully in a stop-start pattern. 'Lankin is fond of a snare or two.'

I try to follow him.

'Hold!' Allison snaps behind me and zaps something about a foot in front of us. A green bubble rises slowly to eye-height. In it is a rusty, brutal bit of kit, caked in hair and blood from however many previous kills. *Bollocks, she's had to save me* again.

I watch as Allison flicks the bubble away. It bounces, one, two, three times before rolling to a stop under one of the windows.

'So, what happens if this feller staggers in pissed one night? Is he on a death wish or what?'

Jack raps on the door, before shrugging his shoulders.

'If a man at the very end of his wit is to kill himself, it would please him not to delay, would it not?'

You can't argue with that logic. I don't know the bloke personally, but if Long Lankin is a killer, you've got to wonder whether there was even any there to begin with. My guts are turning, and every little thing is setting me on edge as we wait for the door to open. The breeze ruffling the trees, Sarah-Jane grabbing my hand without warning – I'm not sure she's too keen on all this, either. Even the *crack* of Allison's foot squashing an acorn makes me jump.

'He might not be in,' I say, hopefully. 'Never mind, we can get to Donald without him, can't we?'

Jack cracks his knuckles, or his twigs.

'Lankin answers, not to just anyone. We've a system – even now I've sent in my messengers to alert him of our presence.'

Shit. Sure enough, there's sound behind the door. A scraping, uneven stomp – heavy boots on floorboards, getting nearer. There's a rattling of chains, the knocking of metal contraptions – heavy bolts unbolting.

The door budges open slightly, but I don't get to see what's beyond. Jack's messengers, hundreds of them, all sizes, swarm the door and are headed right for us. It's spiders, and I'm *out*.

***

The next thing I know I'm lying down somewhere and feeling all cootie, scratching at my arms and face as I feel the little hairy bastards running all over me.

'Get them *off* me!'

Sarah-Jane grabs my hands and forces them to my sides. Something in my shoulder pops indignantly.

'There is nothing on you, Matty. Jack got rid of them all after you fell.'

Even if that's true, I'm still itching all over as I sit up. I can hear a whispered argument in full swing somewhere off to my side.

'But you might have told me the lad had a phobia,' Jack grumbles. 'I could have sent in something fluffy instead.'

'Well, but one would think the spirit of nature would employ not *spiders* as messengers. What of something with fewer legs?'

Fantastic. I've just made a bigger twat of myself than I already am. That, and I'm sitting on what must be a murderer's settee. I give my head one last scratch and take in chez Lankin. It's cosy, at least. Last night's fire is dying in the hearth, enshrined by a wooden mantle, and for being little more than a hole in a muddy bank, it's pretty well rigged out.

133

Everything is made of oak, rough-cut and simply carved – the big chair Allison is sitting in whilst arguing with Jack, who's bent nearly double with the low ceiling; the table and chairs by the window; and the shelves that line the curved walls. On the shelves are hundreds of cute little carved figures, different shapes, creatures and objects alike. It could almost be a lifetime of work for somebody furnishing doll's houses for a living.

Beneath the shelves, on the floor, are more traps and snares, all in different sizes and states of disrepair. One corner of the room is dedicated to wood – a huge pile of logs nearly reaches the ceiling, and a number of axes and knives are stacked alongside. That's maybe the only thing to worry about besides the wolf skin rug on the floor. It's still got its head, but apart from the eyes being removed it doesn't seem to have been treated in any way. It smells meaty. Perhaps it's one of the traps' latest victims.

Sarah-Jane plonks her bum down next to me.

'Stay your quarrel, Allison. This one has awakened!'

Allison huffs and crosses her legs in the chair, giving Jack the biggest of daggers.

'Just as well for you, Jack-maketh-me-Green-about-the-Gills. Had you killed the lad of fright, your natural order would have had never a hope!'

A man's voice cuts through any reply Jack might want to make:

'Enough.'

I crick my neck as I turn to see the man behind me. He doesn't look like your ordinary serial killer, but it must be Lankin sure enough – he's big and hench for his middle age, and nearly seven feet tall. That's got to be "long" in anyone's book. He stoops over me.

'All right, lad.'

It's more a statement than a question, but I still nod. He grunts and stomps over to his table – or rather; he doesn't mean to stomp, but he must weigh quite a bit for his steps to sound that way. He sits down and upturns his hands to the crusty loaf on the table – *massive* hands, perfect for strangling or breaking necks. I don't even feel my own move to my throat, but Sarah-Jane pulls them away.

'If you good people have yet to break your fast, please share in mine.' His face doesn't suit the sentiment. It's sullen, like he's had the worst night's kip ever and really can't be arsed to play host this morning. I guess Jack wasn't kidding when he called Lankin a hermit. I'd feel sorry for the bloke, if it wasn't for his song playing on a loop in the back of my mind. *"There was blood all in the kitchen, there was blood all in the hall."* There's too much evidence in everything that's happened so far not to use that antique material as a warning.

Not that anyone else has taken any notice. They're all gathered around the table, apart from Jack who's now nicked Allison's chair and is sitting picking bits off himself. Spirits of nature don't need to eat, it seems. I do, though. My guts are making squelchy noises that aren't quite rumbles, and I feel sick. The girls are tucking into the killer's bread, and it looks good. Not one of them has dropped down dead yet or has gone purple in the face, so maybe it's not booby-trapped after all. *Whatever.* I get up – a bite won't hurt.

'Cheers,' I mutter, not looking Lankin in the eye. Because

if there's still the possibility it *is* poisonous bread, then his miserable eyes would probably give it away and me punching slices out of the girls' hands would start major drama. And blow any more of that today.

I feel his eyes on me as I chew. Calculating, weighing me up. Spraying my arm with crumbs as he demolishes his own slice. Some of it sticks in his beard. I swallow hard.

Allison's lips smack as she finishes.

'My word, man, you appear to be well versed in the ways of the home. You cook as well as any woman.'

'Aye. One learns what they need to,' Lankin says. *What the hell?* He's still watching me, not even turning to look at what he's doing as he cuts another slice. That much I can see in my peripheral vision. The knife seems way too big for just slicing bread. Is it just wear on the handle, or are those darker areas of wood something worse?

'And which wind of fortune brings you all to me, and in such good company? You'll not go far wrong with Jack by your side. Many's the time he's ensured my survival in the bleakest winter.'

Jack rustles, sheepishly proud, by the fire.

'And many's the time you've helped my creatures, Lankin. Though I fear I must enlist your help again.'

'Aye?' He stops cutting. I wish he'd stop looking at me.

Sarah-Jane, still shovelling it in, elbows me, and I know I've got to meet his eye.

'Jack told us you can take us to Lord Donald,' I say, staring straight at him.

Something in his expression changes. It's there in his eyes

as they widen, in his mouth as it tightens.

Pain shoots through my chest as he shoves me to the wall. His hand is nearly as wide as my chest and pins me down. I can't move.

I can only see the knife.

20
Sandy

Matty Dog and I are wandering around the grounds this morning. Now that Donald's placated Thacks, I'm off scrubber's duty – out of the cold tower, and back to being lady of the manor. He made the old git apologise to me too, for punishing me so harshly and for threatening the dog. I'll never understand that, not with the history between Donald and him. Still, I won't complain. I only hope he can come with me when the time comes to go back. If it comes.

Matty Dog barks at me, snapping me out of it. As if he's telling me to pull myself together and get out of this morbid "if" mindset. If Thacks reckons he's going to kill me on May Day, then that's two whole days to go. And if Matty is on his way for me, well, he can't be too far. I've got to keep busy and take my mind off of potential death, so I can keep hoping.

Walking's nice, especially in these lovely old grounds. I know now that we're in Leeds Castle, and I seriously bloody doubt I'll be renewing my annual membership again after all this. There's only so many times you can chuck sticks for the dog near the lake, so we traipse back up to the castle itself, nipping into the little courtyard where, in the home version Leeds Castle, there's an overpriced café and a brilliant museum of dog collars. I wish Matty Dog could see them, he'd look the nuts in a heavy leather number. Here, though, the courtyard is where all the working animals are kept, and where the horses and pigs and chickens live.

Ellyn's here too. She's bent over a trough, emptying a sack of grub for the pigs into it. She looks even grubbier than usual, and as red as beetroot. Though she's in a better place than Mercy, who's shovelling horseshit onto a wooden barrow, and looks as though she's fallen in it at least once today. *Nice.*

The wooden gate makes a terrible scraping noise against the stone path as I open it, setting all of my teeth on edge. Matty Dog bounds straight through, right at the chickens who scatter and squawk. He won't hurt them, though. He only wants a play. The girls don't bat an eyelid.

'All right, Ellyn? Merce?'

Mercy lifts her spade in acknowledgement, flicking flecks of shit into the air. Some lands on her bonnet. I'm not bothered. I'm not even bothered that she legged it the other night. It's Ellyn I really want to talk to, after she got all upset that time. I want her to know everything's cool. I feel like a girl in one of those old paintings, with a demon sitting on my chest.

'They're enjoying that, eh?' I nod at the porkers tucking into the grub Ellyn's laid on for them, making cute, happy piggy noises. She folds the empty sack over her shoulder and stands slowly, holding her hips. Poor cow's back must be killing her, and it's hardly surprising the way they use her as a skivvy.

'Please, m'lady,' she says, back to me. Bugger, we're back to this "my lady" business again. 'Let me get on with my work.'

'I won't stop you, Ellyn. What's the matter? Why you all mardy, like?'

Her shoulders hunch. I know the movement, the same one Matty does when he's been caught doing something he shouldn't. It's shame, and Ellyn shouldn't feel that way around me.

'I wonder you speak to me so kind, m'lady,' she finally peeps. As she turns to look me in the eye, her mouth has caught up and her eyes are brimming. Christ, what's she got to cry about?

'What you talking about, kind? Ellyn, I'm the one who should apologise to you.'

'But if you had not come with us, you would have been caught not.'

'That's got nothing to do with it. That old prat's got eyes everywhere, I know it. He's magic, isn't he? I should apologise for coming with you, leading him right to you when you were well in there with the boys. I hope I haven't ballsed it up for youse all and getting your leg over.'

That's it. All at once we're laughing again, and the weight on my chest is gone.

'What does it mean, "to balls up"?' Ellyn says.

'The simple version is ruining something.'

'Oh! But you have ruined nothing not, Sandy,' Ellyn says. 'What we servants do outside our hours of labour is of no importance to Thackeray. True, his face was naught but disgust – but who we dally with and how we do it concerns him not.'

'Well, I'm glad for you, Ellyn. That's cheered me up no end.'

Against my better judgement, I go in for a hug. She still reeks to high heaven, but it's overpowered by the stink of Mercy's work and friendship restored, even if it wasn't that buggered to begin with. It's stupid, really, what makes us girls worried, when there are so many more things to worry about in the world. Like getting something to eat. All this country air and walking is great, but it certainly makes you hungry.

'Have you two had any lunch yet?' I ask.

Ellyn cracks up at that and points at a huge mound of hay leant up against the stables.

'Lord, no! I've still to make the horses comfortable once Mercy has done her part.'

'All right. I'll help you, then. Quicker we get done, quicker we can get some grub.'

I go for the iron fork, but Ellyn snatches it from me before I can grab it.

'No, Sandy. The lady of the house labours not.'

'Oh, go out – it was all right when I was helping you out in the kitchen the other day, wasn't it!'

'Aye, but that–'

I take the fork off her.

'Come on, tell me – what d'you want me to do?'

She tells me to start shifting the hay from the mound in the far stable and to chuck a load in each individual stable. It's easier said than done. The fork's heavier than I was expecting, and awkward. Cumbersome. And as for moving stuff with it, it's no good if it all keeps falling off. I carry on regardless, while Ellyn lobs bucketsful of water in the stables that Mercy's cleared.

She's done the other four stables before I've even shifted enough to make one horsey bed in mine. It grates on me when she laughs.

'Sandy, wherefore movest you the hay so? You offer more amusement in your efforts than a troubadour! You hold the tool wrongly, to begin.'

'It's not my fault, though, is it?' I puff. 'Where I'm from, I've never gotten to do any real work. One of the pitfalls of living in a bloody town in the age of convenience.' I chuck the fork and wipe my face in the crook of my elbow. 'But give me a fiddle and I'll show you something that I *am* half good at.'

'You play?' Mercy hollers from her perch on the pig's trough.

'Yeah.'

Ellyn's eyes gleam like somebody from a shoujo anime. I'd laugh if she wasn't so serious. I'm guessing these people don't get much by entertainment with old Thacks about.

'Would you give us a tune?' She nearly whispers it.

'If you like. Just to stop you taking the piss,' I say, and nudge her.

'Here,' she says, picking the fork out of the mini-mound I'd made. 'I shall carry on, if you would fetch some more water. There's a butt just near the chickens.'

I never make it, though. I've only just got the bucket when Matty Dog bounds up to me, barking like a loony and jumping up on his hind legs, towering over me. His big lolloping paws scratch my neck and nearly knock me over with the weight of him. I put my hands on what would be his shoulders and try to force him down.

'Whatever's the matter with you, divvy dog? What are you trying to tell me?' I wince as I say it, twigging exactly how much I sound like a kid from an old-school adventure story. He gets down as Abigail runs, limp and all, into the courtyard, hair and pinny flying, and waving her arms.

'There! Be a man! At the gate!' Abigail manages between chesty pants that sound like asthma. Ellyn sits her down next to Mercy and rubs her back.

'Calm yourself, Abigail. Wherefore did you trouble yourself to tell us only this?'

Abigail shakes her head.

'He seeks employment.'

'That actually happens?' I ask. I feel my head shake in disbelief, because it's always so bloody easy for people in folksong to get work, and never any poxy interviews to navigate.

'It's not another maiden in disguise, is it?' Ellyn says. 'Samuel told me his master has fallen for yet another young widow that came to him in men's weeds.'

'Nay,' Abigail says, her breath finally straightening out. ''Tis surely a real man at that gate. Though one would think even Ellyn has more meat on her bones. He's a thick lip, too.'

The girls carry on chatting, but my mind's in overdrive. I carry on stroking Matty Dog as I try to collect my thoughts. If the guy's thin, and got a thick lip, isn't there a good chance that he could be a fighter? What if it's that swordsman that Thacks mentioned, Matty's friend? What if something's *happened* to them?

FOLKED UP

I wet my lips before asking:
'What's the name of this bloke who's come?'
'I believe he did say it were Taylor.'

21
Matty

The knife doesn't make contact, but it's a bit too close for comfort – held conveniently so that if I move an inch or two either way, it'll cop my eye or my throat. Either way, I'm toast.

'You mention that bastard Donald to me not,' Lankin snarls. '*Not* in my own house, you hear?'

'I hear! I'm *sorry*,' I say, hands up, and I feel his grip on me slacken. It's just enough that my feet meet the ground again, though my legs shake and nearly have me over. 'I think I've pissed myself.'

Nobody tells me otherwise, which is a worry. As soon as Lankin lowers the knife and steps back, I go for a feel. I'm dry as a bone, and it's one tiny victory with all things considered.

Allison stops chewing on the end of her wand.

'Good man forgive me if I am mistook,' she says, as Sarah-Jane grabs my hand. She is shaking to. 'But he spake true. Yon living bush did tell us you could take us to the estate of Don– the *unmentionable*.'

All eyes are on Jack now, balled up once again and looking

as innocent as a bloody houseplant in his chair. He sighs – no, *bounces* – once and grumbles.

Lankin shakes his head.

'He lies.'

'Oh, I'll turn him into *salad*!' Allison screams, eyes wide and finally, *finally* looking like the real witch I met in the tower days ago. Her hair seems to stand on end as she turns her magic on the corner that's full of logs. The whole room feels charged with electricity. Even the hairs on my arms stand on end as the axes, knives and other sharp objects jerk out of the logs and their resting places and gravitate towards the trembling bush on the chair. Snapping and clacking fills the air, making us all jumpy, as the traps and snares open and shut their jaws like a bunch of old women who won't stop moaning at the bus stop.

Even Lankin, mountain man extraordinaire, seems to be impressed by the spectacle. His knife wrenches itself out of his hand and heads for Jack, too, joining the ranks of blades and metal that are floating, slowly but certainly, towards him. One of the windows behind me smashes. None of us look, but the quasi-demonic symphony of baying, moaning, and alarmed chirping beyond means the animals are worried about their master, and have kicked the bloody thing in.

'Allison, hold,' Sarah-Jane says, her voice shaking a bit. It's weird to hear her this scared, and I go cold. 'You cannot mean to really do him harm?'

'Ho! Just you see,' Allison spits, making a winding motion with her wand. Immediately, the sharp things change gear and speed up. 'Spirits are as witches, they are bound to break never a promise! He *deserves* this.'

Jack curls into an even tighter ball as the objects surround his personal space.

'But Lankin!' He hollers over the ruckus. 'You yourself did come from Donald's estate! Were you two not *friends?*'

Silence, now. The knives and axes stop in mid-air. The traps and snares have shut up. The animals sound like they've clammed up, too, even though their shadows still fall over the wolf skin rug. The only sound is Lankin's breathing as he tries to keep from getting more and more pent up.

'That monster may have some friends,' he says. 'I am not one of them.'

This guy has obviously got serious beef with Donald, and I'm pleased that Allison's got the sense to twig it. Her arms spread out wide, like she's drawing invisible curtains. The weapons and other bits of metal glide sheepishly, if that's even possible, back to their places, except Lankin's knife, which lays itself down on the table, next to the bread.

Jack unbundles ever so slightly.

'Thank you, kind witch – *merciful* witch!'

'Hold thy tongue,' Allison spits. 'I'm all but done with thee, *shrub*.'

Ouch. He curls up even tighter. Lankin seems to contract like a mirror image, sitting down at the table with his head virtually in his lap.

'Forgive me good man,' Sarah-Jane says, sitting down opposite him. 'There are many areas where I may be labelled dense, or worse. I know not. Yet prithee, wherefore would Jack bring us here if you could not help us?'

147

'I *am* here, you know!' Jack huffs.

Lankin lifts his head to narrow his eyes at him.

'Aye and would that thou knowest better. Did I not tell thee of my sorrow two years thence? When first I did come to live in this place?'

I know I'll probably regret asking, but I do it anyway.

'What happened?'

22

Sandy

We get to meet this Taylor guy over an early dinner, which is just as well because we never had time for lunch after calming Abigail down and doing the rest of the mucking out. The girls aren't here yet – they've got to take their grub in the kitchen, but I've forced Donald to let them in to "partake" in the entertainment I've been asked to provide. From what I can gather, Thacks isn't too happy about it, the snooty prick. Yet there's still a fiddle next to me, which he obtained for me under duress, and it's comforting to feel the wooden neck under my fingers – like the touch of an old friend – and the warm fuzz of Matty Dog in the other.

I grin at Thacks now across the table. It's not reciprocated, his jaw locked in a sour pout and eyebrows furrowed. I notice they've taken away any sharp or blunt objects from near the fire. From the table, too. *It's a bit late now*, I think, clocking his still-bandaged hand drumming his fingers. They don't even look capable of the torture he inflicted on Matty and me. I feel sick just thinking of it.

A few maids whose names I still don't know bring in the

grub. You'd think these lords would be sick of roast dinners by now. I know I am. I'd give anything for a big greasy Chinese with extra prawn crackers, but they'd probably call me crackers if I asked for it. And bugger trying to explain what a chicken chow mein with crispy chili beef tastes like, besides heaven.

Matty Dog's nose is up on the table, just brushing the edge of my plate, and his ears are standing to attention as one of the maids loads me up with veggies. I scratch his head and reach for the meat.

'You were better to wait for our guest and his lordship,' Thacks warns.

'Like fun am I waiting for him. My tea will get cold,' I say, and help myself to a few slices. 'What are they doing, anyway?'

'Sir Taylor has gone to change. You might learn a thing from him,' he says, wrinkling his nose up. I know he's having another pop at my hoodie and jeans combo, but I'm over all that now.

'So, I'm stuck with you until they rock up, eh?' I say, making sure to have my mouth full as I do. 'Lucky me.'

I stare him out, chewing with an open mouth – and I can't even stand to do it, but, oh, it's so great seeing his face contort and his drumming fingers get quicker and quicker until I think they're going to bore holes in the table. Matty Dog's making the most of the silent stand-off, too – a few bits of chewed-up food go astray, just in reach of his greyish-pink tongue.

It's about to kick off when all of a sudden Thacks stands to attention. I wonder if this guy's got a sixth sense or if he can do magic in his head, because it's a good minute before Donald and his mate, this Taylor fellow, wander in and sit down.

I take a long, hard look at Taylor as he sits down. Could have fooled me if he was changing for dinner, because his shirt's filthy, and hanging on him where he wants a good meat pie to fill him out. He also hasn't cleaned up the thick lip, which is a lot worse than Abigail made out – it's split completely and blooded up into a crust in the dip between his lips and chin. His hair's a state too, coming loose from the little ponytail he's got going on. It's hardly worth him having the ribbon in it still.

'Please, William, help thyself,' Donald tells him. Taylor mutters his thanks and picks up a piece of bread. He nibbles at it gingerly, apparently trying not to set his sore mouth off – or else not wanting to make a pig of himself in front of his would-be employer. I wonder if they've even come to an arrangement at all, because, shallow as it is, he doesn't look like the sort of bloke that would be any use in a lord's household.

It's an awkward meal to say the least. There's not much by way of conversation, and it's not that nobody's trying. Donald and Thacks are asking him all sorts of questions, only to be met with one-word answers. Even the Year Tens and Elevens that came into college one time to look around had more conversation in them, and they were glued to their phones for most of their taster lessons. He doesn't make an awful lot of eye contact, either, and that really is weird given the circumstances.

'From whence do you hail?' Thacks tries after several goblets of wine.

'Lichfield.'

Brilliant! Epic folksong skills strike again. *Bold William Taylor* of Lichfield is having dinner with us and suddenly the

Brummie accent makes sense. Now I'm on safe ground, and I might even be able to strike up a half-decent conversation.

'D'you know, William, I sing about you,' I say, shoving my plate to Matty Dog's tongue zone. Donald leans in slightly when I say this, his face set with full attention.

'My lady?' William says.

'Yeah, and Donald, too. Not so much you, Thacks, because Christ knows what rock you crawled out from. You're not in the club like these two. The *folk* club,' I explain. 'No, you, William and Donald. People will write songs about you. Or perhaps they already have, if we've co-existing timelines or what have you.'

'Yes, Donald mentioned your musical prowess,' William says, a ghost of interest flashing across his face. And that's not weird at all – I bet Thacks has been telling Donald stories about me, the twit. 'Would you give us a song, now? Perhaps mine?'

And I tell him, yeah, I will, but make sure the girls are here because I did promise them and Thacks is sour as anything because of it. And Donald tells one of the maids standing by to fetch her friends while I inspect the instrument he gave me earlier. Matty Dog gives it an inquisitive sniff and wags his great doggy tail slightly before settling down in front of the hearth to watch me tune up. Soon enough, Ellyn, Abigail, and Mercy rock up – they're not allowed to join us at the table but linger behind William and do that nervous excitement shuffle you do when you get to do something naughty, but it's allowed for once. I feel a bit like a minor celebrity.

As I play, it's magic. If just touching the neck under the

table feels like the touch of an old friend, actually having the strings under my fingers and the bow in my hand is comparable to hooking up with your ex and having the best sex you've had in your whole bloody life and wondering why on earth the pair of you ever broke up, because you're perfect together. You feel guilty, and I feel guilty that I've not touched a fiddle in days. I play an old wordless jig at first, *Haste to the Wedding,* and it's only about halfway through as the girls begin to dance that I twig the almost-irony in picking a tune of that name. Why this? Last thing I want to think about now is weddings, especially my own prospective one, and I certainly don't want to haste away to that farce of a ritualistic killing; but the music makes it all right, and the moment passes and I carry on striking the strings and bobbing in time like a girl possessed like Matty always tells me.

It's my life, and right now it's the maids' lives too and I'm so chuffed that they're enjoying this. It's one small pleasure, and they can't get much, not with the way things are here. It makes my enjoyment all the more meaningful. Donald's enjoying himself too, rapping on the table to make an unintentional beat – though I don't care about that any more than I'm pleased of an appreciative audience.

William surprises me as I finish. He leaps to his feet to clap before anybody else gets a look in.

'My word, you've quite the talent!' He puffs.

'Sandy has become wise to the ways of folksong,' Thacks hisses, and shoots me a smug smile. It's a massive "I told you so" sort of smile, as well as a dig at the book. Blow that. There's no way I'm letting him of all people bring me down, not now it's the most I've felt even close to home since I've been here.

'Oh, but William's not heard his song, yet!' I say and try to be cool and give him a wink. It's almost like I'm back on stage. Matty Dog woofs his approval, and before I even get William's, I start:

'I'll sing a song about two true lovers
Who from Lichfield town they came.
The young man's name was William Taylor,
And Sarah-Jane was the lady gay's.
Fie diddle oh hum hi diddle diddle dum,
Fa-la diddle oh hum a day rye day…'

The girls clap this time, as I sing all about the supposed exploits of the man sitting opposite me. It makes me feel just a touch uneasy as he stares at me, his jaw clenching every time Sarah-Jane does something wild like going to sea or chasing him down. I wonder if I'm touching nerves or whether it's a false account of what happened, or because God forbid a song cast a strong spotlight on women in this sausage fest that is Ye Olde England.

I finally reach the verse where Sarah-Jane spots him walking out with another woman and opens fire, but I never get to finish it. She's just called for a pair of pistols when:

'Enough!' William leaps up and kicks his chair, before pointing a spindly finger at me. I stop.

'How come you by this knowledge? How comes it that a girl I have never met knows every single detail about my life, and about the fate of my poor Elspeth?'

'I told you,' I say, putting down the fiddle and heading around the table towards him. 'Where I'm from, future or not, they write songs about your lot! You want to open your ears, you turncoat twat.'

'I beg your pardon?'

I feel my cheeks go red, but I carry on regardless.

'Well, honestly, what sort of bloke goes off to sea and hooks up with another sort while he's got a missus waiting for him indoors? A good missus, one that's ready to leave her life and her family behind and follow you into the Navy just to make sure you're all right because she might actually love you? You're a total bastard, mate.'

That shocks the girls, and him, too.

'Well!' He says, laughing and really riling me now. 'What happens? That's two fools within two score and eight hours that cannot speak the King's English!'

That's done it. Perhaps I'm not the best spoken, all prim and proper, but to me it's normal, and for where I'm from it's normal. But I'm certainly no bloody fool, and this bloke's going the right way for a clump. There are no sharp things around, but I can still try clawing his eyes out. Only I don't get near the prick, because Prick Number One stands up and puts his hands up and I'll have to go through him as well if I have to.

'We'll have no more of this!' Thacks barks. 'The very pair of you – look on the distress you cause your lord and host.'

Donald doesn't look very distressed to me, sipping at his wine and seeming as though he might enjoy a bit of a ruck. I'd do him in, with the mood I'm in. Yet something that William said makes me stop and think.

'Hold on. You said "two",' I say. Matty Dog looks up at me, head cocked as I say it. 'Two fools. Who else have you met who

155

can't talk properly? Do you know Matty?'

That's spooked him, with his eyes wide and mouth hanging limp.

'You must be the girl he seeks?' He slaps the table. 'Well, this is quite something! Had he not gone into that castle–'

'What castle? Is he all right?'

'Aye, I don't doubt it. He's a real band of *powerful*, if idiotic, folk about him.'

Thank Christ.

'That's quite enough of that, sirrah,' Donald says. I see his eyes meet Thacks's, who nods. I so wish that Donald would speak for himself and stop being a puppet all the damn time. 'Forget not the basis upon which we permitted you join us. Your one task.'

William swallows.

'Aye, my lord. And quite right, too.' Something in his mannerism changes, and I can't put my finger on what it is. He sits down like he's got a broom up his backside. Matty Dog must sense it, too – his ears are back, and his mouth curled up in a toothy yet silent snarl.

'Play us another tune, wench,' William says.

'I bloody will not. I'm not just some wench, and, actually, neither are the servants you keep locked in this ridiculous, faux-medieval patriarchy!'

'Oh, Sandy, you mustn't!' Ellyn squeals from by the door, her face twisted up in terror. I put a hand up.

'No, I must. Somebody's got to say it, and it may as well be me. Sod them. After all, I'm the one who's got to worry, aren't I? They can't bloody touch me, not until May Day. Not until Donald marries me, until beardy wanker with the eye *kills* me. Believe me, I've got a whole bunch of things I want to say before then!'

Even I stop, now, as the strangest thing happens. The torches all around the hall which have been glowing warmly throughout our meal, all seem to explode. Jets of fire shoot straight up to the ceiling, one by one from both sides of the hall. The torches explode from the far ends and seem to meet in the hearth behind me. The hearth vomits heat, nearly burning my back. Above it, Benevolence's portrait is bathed in orange, glowing fiercer and fiercer with each torch exploding until it's almost its own light. Bitch be *pissed,* I think, as I struggle to hold Matty Dog back as he's barking like mad.

'Observe, sire!' Thacks spits, clambering around the table to point at the painting. 'Already your lady grows impatient to join us once more!'

Donald doesn't look none too happy, though. He scratches at his little beard with eyes big and as orange as Jaffa Cakes.

'Thackeray, were we better to keep the whole affair here?' He asks, voice low. 'This is the estate she knew, after all.'

'It matters not.'

The torches blaze once more, before dimming down to their old, ambient level of burning. It's then that I realise just how dim and dingy this place really is, despite its grandeur. Matty Dog is still barking like a loony, and I have to hold him to me and stroke his neck to get him to quieten down.

'Say we call off the siege, then?' says Donald. 'It is surely to Benevolence's pleasure that we not tarnish the event with bloodshed.'

157

'What siege?' I say, finally silencing Matty Dog.

'Have you not been told?' William smirks, and I want to smack him and open his wound up even more. 'I'm to watch over this place in the absence of you all. Donald is to take the king's castle at Dover for himself, and you shall have a beautiful wedding by the sea. Most girls dream of such things.'

Bastard.

'But Matty! What if he comes here, instead?'

'Precisely,' Thackeray says, smiling. 'What indeed? Now take that cur and retire to your chamber, there's a good girl. We men have business to attend to.'

23

Matty

We're all ears as Lankin beckons us to come nearer, like a seven-foot beast of a teacher gathering the class for story time at the end of the day. He fiddles with his knife as he seems to struggle getting his words out.

"Tis true, I did have some dealing with Donald, though it feels like a lifetime or more since. I worked on his estate. My wife, Elenore, too – I tended the gardens, and she would oversee the maids' work in the kitchens. His lordship was good to us, then.'

I jar a bit, wondering how the hell a bloodthirsty old git could ever be called "good" in the slightest sense. He swallows hard and carries on.

'He was so good. We lived in lodgings on the grounds of his estate. When Elenore fell pregnant – well, one might say it did please him. Most employers might have cast her out, and I with her, but he ensured her duties were light. Though I am certain his wife had some hand in that – she was barren and looked upon Elenore as her own child. It must have been something of a pleasure for her.'

'His wife – that would be the Lady Donald?' Sarah-Jane asks.

'Benevolence,' he says. 'Yes. She did insist 'pon being present at the birth and did give Elenore such comfort. When Alys, our daughter, was born, so comes it Benevolence did weep more than dear Elenore.'

Allison, I notice, is chewing on her wand again.

'We continued to work and lived happily for two years more. Until Donald employed an adviser of sorts. He was a fiend, and methinks his influence did extend to Donald and poison his mind. Donald would always halve his in-gatherings and distribute one half of that food among the live-in staff. When Thackeray came, it was our good fortune to receive but one meal a day. And where our food diminished, so our workload increased twice over. Donald even forbade Alys from joining my wife in the kitchen, as Benevolence had always permitted.'

'Didn't Benevolence say anything to him?' I ask.

'I believe she did.' Lankin taps his fingers on the knife's handle. 'Methinks my wife was her sole confidante. Elenore would often relay Benevolence's dismay and her concerns to me at home – she did complain that Donald favoured Thackeray's company over his own wife's, and so Benevolence sought solace in my colleague. Matty Groves was the greatest friend a man or woman might have.'

No. No way has some dude here got the same bloody name as me. I wonder if that might have something to do with the workings of the songbook and its alaka-whatsit bullshit. Even Allison shoots me a funny old glance, like this might be

160

important – but Lankin carries on.

'But Matty was a fool. He continued to indulge Benevolence in carnal relations with him and did reveal to her that he would dispatch Thackeray – lest he continue to coerce the master into mistreating the staff. But she was afeared for her husband, afeared that to kill Thackeray would have… *repercussions* of some kind. And so, she did convince her husband to cast us all out – out of employment, and out of home, too.

'Methinks that dear Elenore's heart did break that summer. She grew thin and wan for want of proper nourishment. And for some illness of the mind – in the absence of work, of friendship, she did spend endless days in our temporary arrangement in the village. Alys, too, would cry, piercing howls that made me feel ashamed. I do believe she would have starved to death had she not…'

'Not what?' We all say it at the same time, but I've got a rotten feeling I know what happened to little Alys in the end. There's a horrible dry lump in my throat.

'Matty and I did conceive a plan, when we decided enough was had. 'Twas not the most well-conceived, but by Jove, we had to do *something*. And so comes it that on May Day we did break into Donald's estate by moonlight. Matty had the only weapon between us – a knife that Donald himself had once given him for his services. We sought, without thought, to send that Thackeray to finally meet his maker. Perhaps then would the master see sense and employ our services once more.

'The house was dark, but we knew our way therein. We kicked the door to the scullery full in, and stole through the kitchen, into the servants' backstairs. We moved with never a sound, never any damage made. 'Twas only when we came to the hall that we did hear stirrings above. Nobody could have heard us approach. Yet on the landing, at the top of the stair, torchlight appeared from the passage leading to the master's rooms. We waited, in the shadows 'neath the banister, until we could be sure who came.

"'Ho! Who lingers below?" We heard. It did appear to be the voice of that damned Thackeray, and so we answered.

"'Where's the master of the house?" Matty demanded. And in reply, we heard he did away to London some days ago.'

So, there's got to be some truth in the song, I think to myself, as I think of that bloody call-and-return section that took ages for me and Sandy to master, ready for public hearing. Lankin's face tenses up, and he starts to pull at his hair.

'That was good enough for us – with Donald gone, there was nobody could know who killed Thackeray. We exposed ourselves, then – leapt out from the shadows to confront that bastard. Only 'twas Benevolence who stood on the stair.

'She was shocked as we, and to this day I cannot think how we mistook her voice for Thackeray's. She stood as a statue with a torch from her chamber's sconce in her hand and only her night things on. Yea, we did see relief and horror pass her face at the sight of us. She directed her gaze to the knife in Matty's hand, and I took it from him in haste to put it away.

'Yet I made not enough haste. We saw *him* appear, at the top of the stair, with a wild look about him. He cast a hand toward us and did stretch his fingers, one by one, as if to play a tune on an invisible pipe. Matty let out a bawl as he took

Benevolence in a lock of the head, his arm about her throat and his hand atop her head, hollering that he couldn't move. Benevolence, too, shouted and tried to break free. And I, still with that cursed knife, fought to restrain myself and yelled and cursed. Some force compelled me to inch it nearer to my lady. And so, I watched myself stab that lovely woman, who had been my master's wife, right to the heart. One, two, three times, on and on the knife did plunge as I robbed her, helplessly, of her life, and I watched as her blood spilled out of her body onto my hands and onto the floor. And she looked at me with eyes shining in that torch she had dropped, 'pon the first entry. The corners of her mouth upturned all the same, and she coughed Matty's name, and Matty cried as he held her still in that deadly pose and she turned her head t'ward him as best she could and kissed him that one last time as her body and spirit were divided.

'And all the while we knew that bastard had done it, that same villain that now cried "Murder!" and cast his hand towards us again. In so doing, control of our own bodies did return. Matty's returned first, and he dropped her. She fell upon the stair, but the knife still in her chest did bring me down upon her. I tried, in vain, to pull it out, and through the wetness I saw Matty, his own cheeks moist, stumbling t'ward me and telling me to make haste.'

Lankin's crying again now, as he pauses, still pulling at his hair. I don't think this is something he's used to telling.

'Thackeray did lie to us. As I regained control of my limbs, there came the most terrible, guttural cry from the landing. There stood Donald, not in London at all. Merely a pawn in a terrible game that ensnared us all, who saw only that which Thackeray had planned for him to see. Matty and I, two murderers. We ran as we had never run before, out of the estate, into the grounds, t'ward the village. Alas, we were too slow. Cries and the thunder of hooves from behind provoked us to hide by the wayside. The village was in view, and Matty and I... we watched Donald and his servants, who had once been our friends, burn the whole lot down.'

I don't want to say it, to confirm what I'd thought all along. Sarah-Jane is brave enough, even if she's twisting the chain around her neck so much that it might snap.

'Then... Elenore and Alys?'

'Perished. Sure, we did pursue the men once their intentions were plain but proved too late. We returned to flame and corpses. They passed in the arms of one another, in front of the house that had taken us in. So comes it they had escaped the building, and Donald himself did set the pair afire – first Alys, then Elenore as she tried to save her. Thackeray took the most perverse delight in telling me when we arrived. Even now, I hear his laugh, echoing over and over in my head, as a ghost may walk the same route night after night.

'I tore a lump of timber, still aflame, from the house, and lashed at Thackeray atop his horse, missing every time. Methinks I did do him some damage with the embers, for he yelled and clawed at one eye when it passed close by his face. Donald came then, to survey what had happened, and so I fled lest he do by me what I had done by Benevolence. I hid in a burnt-out house, and through my eyes cried dry I saw one of the serving-men bring Matty to him. He was bloody from fisticuffs, and black with smoke – methinks he did go to see if his landlord had survived the burning. The serving-man threw Matty to the ground before Thackeray, who did reveal to Donald his carnal relations with Benevolence. I thought I would see yet more death, and I do believe he would have come for me had that come to pass. I still wonder if it had been the better option than to live this hellish existence.'

'It pains me to hear you say these things, Lankin,' Jack says, in the corner, and brushing at his leafy cheeks. 'All life is a gift. I had never an idea that all this came to pass in this way.'

'Aye, and more to come. They did not kill Matty, despite his plea that he was sorry to have dallied with Benevolence, and if they were to kill him they were better have it over and done with and deliver justice swiftly. Donald exclaimed that he'd devised a special kind of punishment for him. And I do swear to Jove that I saw that same Thackeray, adviser to Donald, mutter to himself before lifting an arm out t'ward Matty and turn that human man into a dog.' Lankin shakes his head like he still can't believe it, as we just sit and try to take this rollercoaster of a story in.

'What manner of dog did they make him?' Sarah-Jane asks.

'Christ's sake, like it matters!' I tell her. Because even though I'm curious myself – because I think of Sandy's dog Ozzy and how I'd take him home myself because dogs are dogs and better than people ever can be – this bloke has just described transfiguration magical bullshit. I really hope this Thackeray hasn't touched Sand.

'I know not,' Lankin says, shrugging. 'I do believe I were too stunned to recollect which breed they might have made of him. And yet I remember his lessening body sprout hair grey as a stone, and his face elongate into a muzzle as though a man had clutched at his face and stretched it. 'Twould have been the greatest horror I had ever seen, were it not for Elenore and Alys.'

The girls are almost in tears with all of this, and I think I'm about to join them and continue the trend in which I make myself out to be some sort of sentimental idiot. And I know that's a rotten way to look at things, because here's this big old woodsman crying and no doubt still suffering from PTSD that's gone undiagnosed all this time because the doctors seem to be few and far between in this place.

'Mate, you really loved Elenore, didn't you?'

'Aye,' he says. He digs at his eyes with his knuckles, driving them in like he's trying to erase the memory as well as dry them. 'So many nights have I sat here with never a houseguest but my own thoughts, wishing I could undo what had been done. Jack has been kind to me, sure, keeping the seasons at bay while I built this hiding-place, and ensuring some of his animals, either old or ailing, would wander into my traps to keep me from hunger. Yet this is only an existence – my life without Elenore and Alys is worthless.'

Jack shrugs in the corner, mumbling about how he does what he can for good men of the forest or what have you, and Allison's look towards him loses a bit of the dagger's edge.

'No life is worthless, Lankin,' Sarah-Jane says, almost in a whisper. She looks at the ring on the chain around her neck, rolling it between her fingers as she no doubt thinks about that douchebag of a husband.

'She's right,' I say. 'And you can do something great if you help us. I thought you were meant to be a murderer, but you're really not, you're actually pretty decent –'

'Thank you?' Lankin says, his face looking like he's tasted something, and he doesn't know whether he likes it or not.

'No, what I mean is – you can be wrong about people. You're wrong about *yourself*. If you can help us, show us to Donald's gaff, you'll have done something worthwhile. Sandy is *my* Elenore – I can see that now. Christ knows why it took all this magic to work that out, and why these two bloody *legends* of women want to help me, but I need to get her back. I need to save her. Will you help us?'

Somebody squeezes my shoulders, and it's Allison doing a sneak attack from behind. She smells earthy, like beetroot, but with a hint of musky perfume. It's mumsy, in a weird way. All of a sudden, I feel like I've done something half-decent, and she approves. Perhaps I have.

'Your quest is noble, Matty,' Lankin says. 'But I cannot help you.'

'You need see Donald not,' Sarah-Jane says. 'If you will only show us a way to him, as Jack suggested…'

'Mention me not! After all, I am but fit for a salad,' huffs Jack. He picks a handful of brown leaves from under his armpit and scatters them on a table, trying to make a point.

'Allison was only taking the mick,' I say. 'Weren't you?'

She sighs and scratches her temple with her wand. No comment whatsoever. Then, for the first time, I see Lankin crack a smile. It suits him. He doesn't look half as terrifying.

'The edge of the estate, then,' he says. He coughs as he

stands up, putting the knife safely away in a pouch hanging on his belt. 'I'll not venture further than that.'

24

Matty

Lankin's cottage had seemed well tucked away in the thickest, darkest part of the wood when we came across it. Now, though, I realise it was just bloody well-hidden. We walk for perhaps twenty minutes, tops, as we dodge fallen or misshapen trees and stumble in animal holes hidden in the undergrowth. Or rather, Sarah-Jane and I do the stumbling, because Lankin and Jack must have walked this route a million times and know the whereabouts of every other rock and toadstool. I'm not sure Allison has, but some witchy premonition of hers must be keeping her from making a tit of herself.

'Confound it, bloody things!' Sarah-Jane says somewhere behind me.

'I don't think I've ever heard you say "bloody",' I say, grinning a little bit because I know she's gone for the same hole I nearly did my own ankle on.

'Aye, your influence reaches us all, Matty,' Allison says. "Tis not positive, either, with your queer profanities and your *badasses* and all, forcing their way into our vernacular.'

'I can't help the way I talk,' I say, stepping over what might be a rock covered in lichen. 'You want me to keep my gob shut, that it?'

'Your so-called "gob" has brought you naught but trouble, has it not? Perhaps t'would not be too bad an idea after all,' she says. I don't know if she's joking, because she shoots me a sly, sort of joking look that might be bants or might be sarcasm.

Ahead of us, Lankin stops, his hand on a tree trunk like he's an explorer scouting the territory. It's the edge of the forest.

I shake my head.

'Were we seriously this close to being out of the woods? We could have walked it yesterday!'

'As I recall, our priority yesterday was to be well rid of yon castle ghost,' Allison says. 'Besides, you learned a thing or two about swordplay, did you not?'

'Allison, this isn't a plot point. This is all about me finding Sandy alive and getting us back home as quick as we can.'

'That may soon come to be, Matty,' Lankin says, interrupting us all. 'Come and observe.'

So, we do, each lining up next to Lankin to have a look. Below us, a great rolling hill spreads out, painting everything in eyeshot that's not the sky a patchwork of green. It seems to sparkle in the morning sun, and I guess it must be earlier than I initially thought. About a mile or so just ahead looks like what might be actual civilisation – a collection of buildings that might make up a village. And further still, a castle or some grand house that looks really bloody familiar, and I've no doubt Sandy's brought us here in the other England before now. It almost feels like I could be nearly home, like the next junction on the motorway is the one I want for home. If there was a motorway, that is.

'That's Donald's place?' I nod my head towards the nearly familiar building.

'Aye,' Lankin says, almost whispering. 'The village is… different.'

But he just clears his throat, and starts walking, not even gesturing for us to follow him. If anybody was going to stop, I'd have thought it would be him. Instead, it's Jack who holds back.

Allison tuts.

'What ails thee, sir?'

'I fear I cannot leave this wood,' he says. He whacks himself on the head twice, and two acorns tumble out of what would be his nostrils. 'The fabric remains unmended, and I must ensure my creatures are safe.'

'Oh, mate. That's really nice,' I say, feeling more guilty than ever.

He shrugs and reaches up into a hollow in the tree next to him. His squirrelly mate runs out, twisting around his arm to sit on his shoulder.

'I do hope you find your ladylove, Matty. For your sakes, and for everyone's.'

He smiles and nods slightly in a very "this is goodbye, but I hope we'll catch up later" way. We do the same, save for Sarah-Jane who bows, and he turns away, whispering to his squirrel as he walks back into the forest to do his thing. What an absolute legend.

171

FOLKED UP

***

Lankin took legs, and it's taken us just more than a brisk walk to catch up with him. He'd stormed towards the village, though I'm not sure why he was in such a rush until we get there.

They've rebuilt everything since the fire, so it looks like a half-decent village; but they've left whatever remained of the burned buildings to the mercy of the seasons. Every few houses or so, there'll be the ghost of a structure sandwiched between actual ones. He lingers by each one, maybe wondering if it was once his place or not. It's taking longer than it should to walk through, and I'm debating whether or not to ask him to hurry his arse up or whether he wants to be left in peace now that the endgame is in sight. It doesn't help that we're getting many weird looks from the people who live and work here. There is pointing and whispering, and a few who even cross their arms against their chests and rush inside. I really don't like it.

'Not one soul has bid us welcome,' Sarah-Jane says, crossing her arms as she walks. 'Most uncustomary.'

'Thank Christ. I thought it was just me. What's the deal?' I ask, hand on my sword just in case anyone tries to jump me.

'Ah, now I fear this may be my fault,' Allison says, clenching up her eyes like she's trying to force a massive dump. It's that "crap, I've just remembered something terrible, and it's gonna screw us all up" face. 'Some months past, I did venture up this way in search of dragon's bile.'

I freeze.

'Are there *dragons* in this place, too?' Because if there are

172

then why the hell couldn't Allison just magic one up and torch the two old bastards?

'Cursed crows, no!' She giggles, and the witchy sound sends a man working a forge running inside. 'Dragon's bile is but a trade name for tree sap. I was in want of some for a remedy. Old Mother Meredith of the Chislehurst Caves had come down on a visit, and she'd a terrible curse put upon her by an especially vile witch. Brought her out in terrible oozing sores, it did. Oh, how we did both abhor that bitch. I believe she lives down a hole in Somerset, now.'

She starts fiddling with her cloak fastening.

'But, forgive me, I ramble. So, it came to pass that the apothecary here, and I had an altercation of sorts when I requested my dragon's bile. He would serve me not, on the grounds that I am what I am, and he feared the besmirching of his business.'

'And?' Sarah-Jane asks.

Allison pulls her top lip into her mouth with her teeth before blowing her cheeks out, like she's calculating what she wants to say.

'I shall spare you all the details. But I may have uttered some words in anger and turned him into a pig.'

I shoot Sarah-Jane a look and we piss ourselves laughing. Allison's just staring at us, serious as you like, which only makes us laugh harder.

'Guess none of us had better get ill, then!' I say, nudging Sarah-Jane.

'This is not a game, Matty. Do you not realise that these people now fear me? All I wanted was that dragon's bile, and

173

as it is poor old Meredith suffers still, for I was not able to help her. I continue to be marginalised on account of my sex and my trade.'

I think back to when I first met her, and how she said she was lonely, and I feel a bit of a prick because she's right and she doesn't deserve that. All the same...

'You did turn him into a pig, though,' I say, running my fingers over the handle of my sword.

'Very well, clever sir – what wouldst thou have done?'

'Friends, please stop your quarrel,' says Sarah-Jane. She nods towards Lankin, who's stopped dead in front of a square patch of ground. It's dead, in the most literal sense. Where the ground behind it has things growing in it, along with intermittent grass, this is just mud with a couple of weeds sticking out of it. It's not been turned over for some time. I think we all know that this must be Lankin's old gaff, where they all went when he was sacked.

'Listen, mate, d'you want to stop and stay behind? We can go from here,' I say, not knowing what else I can actually say. He doesn't answer me at first, he just stands there staring, eyes glazed over, like a kid ogling the coolest toy in the shop and knowing he can't have it. Ever. It's a bit weird, given his size.

'Nay,' he says, his voice thick. 'I had not yet returned to see the place since it happened. 'Tis... smaller than memory would have me think.'

He swallows and turns to look at me.

'I have made it this far. 'Twould ease my sore heart to see lovers reunited. Perhaps it may pre-empt what awaits me when the time comes for me to cross over to the other world.'

'That's a bit morbid, isn't it?'

'Quite the reverse – it is a comfort. Let us press on to Donald – 'tis still a fair walk to the estate,' he says, not giving his old home a second glance.

***

One of the best things I've found about this place is that people do stick to their word. Lankin could have chickened out, made his excuses and left us to go into Donald's estate alone, but he's stuck with us, through the village and beyond – through the unmanned gatehouse that bridges the surrounding lake, past the servant's little abodes and the stables, and right up to the front door. It's not half as grand or scary as I'd expected – it's just a lovely old building. And most definitely goes by the name of Leeds Castle in our place, just as Henry said it would be. Many's the time I've been dragged around the version we've got at home, what with Sandy wanting to make the most of her annual membership. I wonder if it's the same to how I remember it inside, whether these buildings that are shared across worlds have the same general make-up, or whether there are slight differences where the universes overlap. It makes me wish I had more time to explore.

There are no doorbells here, only a big iron knocker in the middle of the wood. It's in the shape of a green man, with vines from his mouth forming the knocking ring part, and I wonder if this is taking the piss. It could be a replica of the one on the front of the book, but in metal and not in leather. Now I'm here, looking at it, and thinking about everything that's happened, everything that could still happen and how it's all the fault of the book. I hesitate to even touch the thing. My hands are shaking, and the palms are sweating like they do when I watch videos of mad people climbing skyscrapers on the Internet.

Sarah-Jane does the honour for me. She tuts and says something that doesn't register, because I'm just stood like a dummy, before reaching out in front of me and giving three hard knocks of the vines. The sound seems to thunder through the house, and through me too, vibrating my chest like the bass drum at a metal concert.

We all stand in silence for the reply, not even looking at each other. Lankin's still here, standing right alongside us, but I can hear his breathing getting more and more shallow, mirroring my own. Out of the corner of my eye, I can see Sarah-Jane's fingers dancing over her sword's hilt in her belt, and even Allison doesn't have any sarky comments. It's because this is it. This is why we're all here. This is how we've all become friends of some kind, and it's all led up to this. It's exciting, and it's terrifying. Why the hell are they taking so long to answer the door and who will it be that answers?

After what seems like ages, the door sighs open, and a young woman in a dirty cloth bonnet steps out. With my legs still not wanting to move, I step forward and clear my throat.

'I'm here for Sandy,' I say in my official voice. The same voice I use to complain when the pizza delivery is late.

The girl nods and opens the door wider.

'Please step in.'

25
Matty

The girl took us through the entrance hall, down past the staircase that Lankin described – he hesitated to go by – and to the left into a fair-sized hall. It's quite cosy despite its height, with a fire going and the tableware glittering in its light and that of the torches. Lankin hasn't taken his eyes off a painting hanging over the fire, a woman in green with long hair hanging down. It's got to be Benevolence. All of a sudden, I start to shit myself at the thought of what might happen if Donald comes in and sees Lankin, like a ghost or a bad memory come to taunt him. I guess at least this time he's got us on his side.

'If it pleases you, my lords and my lady, do quench your thirst with anything from the table. I shall go and fetch the master.' The girl bows her head slightly and then hurries out of the room.

Allison inspects a goblet and then reaches out for a gold decanter.

'Here, it might be poisoned,' I warn.

She tuts and pours herself a generous cup.

'I know a poisoned wine, Matty. I can smell one across a chamber.'

Even if that's true, I'm not liking the idea that she might get half-sloshed before we even get to talk to anyone. Lankin, I've noticed, is silent, and I just know he's wondering whether or not he's done the right thing in coming with me. He really is a good bloke at heart. When I get back, the first thing I'm doing is writing him his own song that puts everything right. People need to know the truth. Maybe I'll even write one about this whole ordeal once we're all home safe. Maybe even a book.

We sit in silence for a while, Allison just drinking and staring at Sarah-Jane, who's building a precarious tower of goblets and other tableware. I watch her, her little hands are placing everything delicately and her tongue sticking out like a kid concentrating on their colouring in. I do wonder how anybody can be so ignorant that they just assume she's a guy because of her short hair and breeches when she is so obviously a petite, gamine woman. I guess it's what you're used to.

The tower's about as high as a chair when the girl returns. A man follows her, a skinny guy with a bit of a bruised face. It looks like –

'William!' Sarah-Jane leaps up, nearly taking the tower with her, and clamps her hand on her sword. Even in the dim light, I can see her face go red. 'I'll not hear a bloody word of what you have to say, not one! How dare you come and work here, of all places, after we had sworn to help Matty!'

'*You* swore, dear Sarah-Jane,' he says. Then he sniffs. 'You still have yet to assume the dress that best becomes your sex?

You have no need of a man's vestments, now.'

'I should have killed you, along with your whore!' She springs forward, but Lankin grabs her arms from behind and holds her there, solid. She struggles, kicking and convulsing like something out of a cheap horror film.

'You would hurt your friend's cause by spitting insults? Methought you had more sense,' he says, sitting down at the far end of the table. She stops and hangs her head. Lankin lets go, and she shrugs him off, slumping down in a chair and crossing her arms. For once, I speak up.

'Listen, I don't care that you're here, or even what you're here for . I couldn't give two shits about it, really, mate. You're nothing to me. I just want Sandy. Please, you know that. Where is she?'

I'm glad I'm sitting down, because everything's shaking. I put my hands on my lap under the table, just so he can't see.

'Alas, your ladylove is not here,' says William.

'You what?'

'Yea, verily, what mean you to say?' Allison pipes up. I don't like this. She knows so much, and now she sounds as uncertain as that awful feeling in the pit of my stomach.

William avoids everyone's gaze, fixing his firmly on the painting above the fire. The expression in the woman's face seems changed somehow – she seemed to be smiling when I first looked at her, and now the firelight throws shadows that make her look sad, almost disappointed. It's ridiculous, I know it is, because paintings don't change unless you're in a fantasy novel, but even just that makes me feel like something's off about the whole thing. It's not right.

'Tis a pity, for they departed this place not three hours thence. Sandy, Lord Donald, Thackeray, and most of his staff, all on horseback, and bound for the coast. So little time, and yet thou standest never a chance of catching up to them.' William smiles and folds his arms. 'Never a chance.'

The smug face is doing me right in, and it's all I can do to stop myself from going around the table and running him through with the sword.

'Where've they gone? Where are they taking her?'

'And methought the news would spread like fire. They are bound for Dover, and to King Henry. So comes it did occur to my lord to overthrow the king, and to be married to Sandy in the castle. So comes it she will meet her end not long after. 'Tis but a matter of hours.'

There's a sting behind my eyes, and I feel like I want to chuck my guts up. That's literally where we were, yesterday, with the trials and the dinner and the ghost, and it's taken us all this time to get here just to find that out. It's over. It's *done*. He's right, we'll never make it in time.

'You know what? You're a right dickhead, William.'

I slam my sword down on the table, making everyone jump. I make to walk out but hear somebody shuffling behind me.

'Matty, hold. My employer asked that I give you *something* to help you on your way.'

I turn around, expecting a sarky laugh or some snidey comment. Instead, I cop a punch up the throat. Everything goes white. I stumble backwards, nearly choking on my tongue, only just hearing cries from the table.

'Matty! Get up not, I've a spell –'

'Where's your honour, man?'

'Jove strike me dead if I should not kill thee, William!'

I just don't care anymore. Struggling to breathe, and with tears coming, I leg it out of there.

26
Matty

I've messed it all up. It's all been my fault, even from the start. I made Sandy feel like she had to read from the book, made her come here to this stupid bloody place, and now I've got her killed, any minute now. There's only one thing left for me to try, to try and get this all reversed – because if *I* die here, surely that'll throw the curse off kilter and send her back through the way she came? Who knows, it might even save me, too. Only before I do that, I'm going to get completely rat-arsed because I can.

There's no drinking age here, and why would there be when you're not likely to reach middle age, anyway? Still sore, I went back to the village where there was a tavern of some kind – there were barrels outside and loud happy noises coming from inside. I don't even question why none of these people are at work – there's a Maypole just next door, and you just know it's *that* holiday. Figures.

I don't have any money to pay, but that doesn't seem to bother the landlord when I go in. Instead, he cheers and says something about visitors being welcome, and I may have as many as I like because summer has begun, and we must all be able to share in the bounty of nature. By which he means the ale, I think. Either way, he slides a scummy leather tankard my way and everyone cheers.

'Wherefore hast thou journeyed here, traveller?' A woman with her breasts threatening to spill out onto the bar tries to cuddle up to me, but I just shrug and sit on a small bench in the corner. The ale tastes like shit, but I carry on downing it, anyway.

A force knocks it out of my hand, and nearly breaks my fingers with it. The tankard flies across the room and I'm looking up at the twisted, sweaty face of Sarah-Jane all up in my grill.

'What thinkest thou? Dover be in the other direction to this place,' she says, hands on the table and leaning into me.

'So what? It's not like I'm gonna make it in time, is it?'

She lifts her fist and slams it into the table. Probably holding back from my face, that'll be the next thing.

'But you must try! You can drink yourself into oblivion, Matty, but I shall be damned if I be the one to allow it. Sandy needs your help!'

'But what is she to you, eh? It's hopeless! Can't you bloody backwards people get that into your heads?'

She stands back, quick, like she's just had a close look at a snake and it's hissed at her. Her eyes narrow. It can't be good, and I'm in for it.

'What did you call me? Say it again, cur, go on.'

'You heard.' Then I laugh. 'You're all backwards, all bloody doo-lally in the head.'

'Well, how do you bring this upon yourself, Matty?' She spits on the floor and chucks something down on the table in front of me. My sword. She takes her own out, and everybody in the place kind of steps back, talking in hushed voices.

I shake my head.

'I'm not gonna fight you, Sarah-Jane.'

'You think me backwards – come! Prove how backwards I am,' she says, smiling ever so slightly as she twirls her own sword like a baton. I just stare at her.

'Well, you are nothing but a yellow-bellied cumber-world after all. I thought better of you, Matty.'

Right in the bloody heart. She turns to leave, but I grab her hand.

'All right, but we do it outside, yeah?'

That seems to be okay by her. I swear I see her smile as she turns to walk out, and I follow her. I grab the landlord, his bald head all sweaty because he obviously doesn't want any aggro, to act as a sort of ref as we head outside. I think that's what you're meant to do.

Allison and Lankin are out there, too, puffing as they've obviously tried to catch up with Sarah-Jane and stop her doing something stupid. Something like this. Allison shakes her head as we keep our swords at our sides and bow at each other, like Sarah-Jane taught me. I've a feeling she's going to put me through the whole rigmarole. It could get ugly, but what does it matter if I'm only going to top myself later on, anyway?

'This has certainly escalated quickly,' Allison tuts, almost reading my mind. She puts her hands on her hips. 'Where are your brains, the pair of you?'

A crowd has gathered now, and the landlord fights his way through to mediate.

'Gentlemen,' he addresses us, which obviously sets Sarah-Jane off with the eye-rolls. They just don't see women out of dresses here. 'I shall speak to you plain – I do not like blood. I will not even watch my own being let by the barber-surgeon. Must you really engage in this?'

'There is a point to be made, sir,' Sarah-Jane says, daring him to say something because if he does then he's bloody well in for it.

The landlord swallows, loudly.

'Very well. Do what you will.'

I brace myself, the sword heavy in my hands, knees bent like she told me. She also bends her knees, and hops from foot to foot. It's like neither of us wants to be the one to start it.

'What think you, little Matty Groves? Be you naught but a yellow-bellied cumber-world? Do you admit that and bring this foolish display to an end?'

I cringe. Nobody's called me "little" Matty Groves in a while, but it still rubs me up the wrong way. It's like she knows it, and I wonder if Allison's said anything to her.

'Little Matty Groves! Little Matty Groves!' She sings, full of glee, as she inches towards me.

It's too much, and there's no way she's getting the first one in – so I charge ahead and bring my sword down. She blocks it, just, and soon we're at it for real. Something inside me has just snapped, and I need to wipe that smug look she has clean off her face, if only to prove that I'm not little and I'm not about to let her beat me.

FOLKED UP

This takes her by surprise – her face is all shock as we spar in the middle of the crowd. They're all cheering, for nobody in particular, just for the pair of us, maybe because it's something different for them to see. Now I know what it's like to be one of the gym wankers in the town centre on a Saturday night when they've been hoofed out of the club and started on someone who was looking at their bird when they were queuing up. I bet their fights were never exactly like this, though. They never had swords, for one thing.

Pain shoots through my arms each time I block Sarah-Jane, and she's throwing in moves we didn't even cover when she was teaching me – the crafty, bloody cow. It's good, though, and if I wasn't so sure that she's not likely to kill me, because we're sort of friends, it would be a bit scary. She plunges her sword towards my crotch, but I block it and force her back into the crowd. They quickly shift, and I've got her – pinned up against the side of the tavern, one hand on the blade and the other on the handle, pressing into her breastbone with the flat edge of the blade.

'Not bad,' she puffs. I swear she smiles, and without even thinking I ease up a bit, thinking that's the end of it all. Instead, she stamps on my foot.

'That's not fair!' I holler as I chase her. She's belted off, past the crowd, and runs up a hen house outside a shop of some kind. I think she's going to do a sly one and come at me from above, so I zip straight past the henhouse. She must twig, because she launches herself over a roast hog that two blokes have just brought out of the shop, into a forward roll towards me. I go for an overhead swing, but she leaps up and blocks it

186

just in time. Pain shoots through me as I reel back.

'You silly cow – did that hurt you as much as it did me?'

'Aye,' she shouts, raining sword-strokes on me now. 'The impact kills me every time – and yet we continue, do we not? Because we let nothing deter us from our goal!'

I know what she's getting at. This is a point that she's trying to make; that I shouldn't give up and that we should try to get to Sandy regardless of whether we'll make it or not, but it's no use. We're both too geared up, in that fighting mode, to stop. The crowd's followed us down the road, and I can hear Allison calling for us to stop and that enough is enough, but still we carry on, deaf to everything but the metallic swishes and clangs.

'It's pointless!' I shout, diving for her and missing. I smash into a shop front and feel my ribs jump up into my chest as the wood windowsill winds me. I roll over, slowly, onto my back, expecting her to come at me again. She doesn't. She just stands there, puffing, but her face looks like she might break out in tears any minute. I really hope she doesn't, because with me feeling like shit both inside and out, I might just join her. I chuck my sword and wipe my forehead.

'It's so pointless,' I say, getting up slowly. 'And you know it. How the hell am I meant to get to Dover in time?'

'But you must *try*, Matty,' Sarah-Jane says. 'And you have. Do you not see how you make me sweat from your efforts at swordplay? You did struggle so in the skirmish with Henry's men, and now you can hold your own? You learned how, for *Sandy*. Do you not see that we all have helped you be where you are, all because we believed that you might really save her?

Do not undo all that has been done. Be not selfish.'

That's done it. With all my back up, I pick up my sword and point it at her, and she hops back.

'I'm not bloody selfish!'

'Look, just pack it in, the pair of you!' Allison shouts. I look at her. She's biting desperately at the fingers of one hand and got her wand in the other, poised ready like she's going to cast some shit on us if we go at it again. *God, she doesn't* really *think I'm going to hurt Sarah-Jane, does she?* Just thinking that makes me feel like scum. I don't want to sink that ship.

I look at Sarah-Jane, biting the inside of her cheek like a kid who's done wrong and looking all sheepish at Allison. Then she sighs and sticks her hand out for me to shake.

'Truce?' I say.

'Aye,' she says, pulling me into a great big hug. It's nice, after everything. Sometimes it's all you need.

I hear loads of clapping as I squeeze her tight, right in close to my chest. There're even a few people cheering, and I feel myself get enveloped by Allison and Lankin as they get in on this free love lark. I want to cry because only proper friends cuddle like this and I've never been lucky enough to be in the middle of one.

'Let's get going,' I say, still in the sandwich.

'Aye, come – I know a man that may help us,' Lankin says. I snap my head back and eye him up – it can't be another one from the back catalogue, can it? But Lankin only smiles down at me.

27

Sandy

The one good thing that's come out of this day is that there wasn't much of a siege to be had when we did actually get to Dover Castle. I'd had visions of Donald's men getting me up before the break of dawn and us all riding down there, armies joining us on the way, for an epic battle against another load of soldiers in full armour, but there wasn't any of that. In fact, there were only twenty or so of Donald's lot, and fewer of them – only King Henry and a handful of courtiers, who gladly turned the king over to Donald. They were raving about a ghost or something and told us we were welcome to the castle.

'Some right-hand men you proved thyselves to be!' Henry hollered as his men scarpered. 'You would leave your king alone, at the mercy of one who would usurp him! And thee, Donald – do what thou wouldst with me. Should you harm my dogs, though, be wary for I shall be revenged on your entire parcel of rogues!'

I never heard what happened after that. I got ushered away into a little room to get myself ready for the wedding. I've been going potty ever since, sitting here just staring at that bloody vile green dress that Thackeray must have picked out for me, because I've a feeling that Donald must have a bit more taste. At least I've got Matty Dog with me.

He shakes himself up now, as someone comes in. It's Ellyn, who must have been attending to some other castle-y duties. She's not turned out too bad and has got some white dress on that's not her usual woolly thing with an apron. Her bridesmaid's rig-out. Despite that, I'm not half pleased to see her.

'Sandy,' she says, doing a curtsy as she comes in. 'You are not quite ready.'

'You think I'm getting married in that thing?' I say, nodding at the dress on the chair. 'Or at all, for that matter?'

She shakes her head, and strokes Matty Dog. He licks his lips and nuzzles into her, and I wonder if he ever knew her when he was a human.

'I know you speak sense, Sandy. And I thank you for your defence of the girls and I yesterday. You so lovingly describe your world. I long to see it, and its fair treatment of all.'

I grimace, thinking there are still fair few things we haven't got right despite being more advanced, but nod because I know what she's getting at.

'Yet we are in this world, and 'tis one dictated at this very moment by Thackeray. We must abide by those rules,' she says, picking up the dress. 'I am instructed to prepare you for the wedding.'

Her voice cracks on the very last word, and she starts full-on crying, snot and all. I don't get it. I'm the one who ought to be ready to blub, but I'm the one comforting her now, hugging her tight as she spasms into my collarbone. I think she might have had a bath ready for the occasion, because she doesn't smell half as bad as she has. Unless I'm just used to it by now. We're there for a good solid minute, just hugging in silence. Like the enormity of everything is going to straight up swallow us whole. I know I wish it would.

'I am sorry,' says Ellyn, once she's able to make sentences again. She means sorry for a number of things for sure, but I get what she must really mean. It's a pity sorry. She's sorry that I'm going to have to die and there's nothing either of us can do about it. I reckon that's the danger when you make friends with people – sooner or later, you'll end up apart. Communication wanes, so I heard from some uni people who came into college to talk to us about the future, but sometimes people die off. That's life, and there's really nothing to apologise for in that. This whole thing may just be the way it has to be. It's worth a shot, and maybe it'll even be my ticket back home.

'Don't be,' I say, shrugging off my hoodie. 'I *get* it.'

Ellyn looks grateful and undoes the dress ready for me to step in. I slip my t-shirt off and she gasps. Loudly. I'm about to turn my back, thinking that it's bad manners to strip in front of somebody else here and I'd better watch myself, but instead I jump when I feel her skanky hands on my waist. They're cold, and I feel her breathing on my stomach. She's examining me like a painted lady at an old-time freak show.

'Sandy, what is this vestment 'cross your bosom? And how do you get the jewel to embed in your navel? And wherefore?'

'Oh!' I crack up and point at my girls. 'You don't have this thing yet. This is something from the future, and it's called a bra. Stops you getting all saggy when you get old and that.'

'Lawks! And the jewel?'

'That's my belly bar. It's a piercing. You can get anything pierced where I'm from.'

'Piercing.' She tries the word out in her mouth. "Tis a shame to keep such a gem covered so! Why, look how it reflects the light!'

'Go out, it's only from Claire's. I got it in the sale with the last of my Christmas money.'

'I wish I could have one,' she says, still staring at my belly. It's a bit off-putting, especially as I haven't had a chance to sort my snail trail lately. She doesn't seem to notice that. 'You must be a grand lady indeed to possess such a jewel! And money for Christmas! 'Tis but another day of the year to me.'

I feel myself smile. Ye Olde Christ's Mass. No worries about writing cards to all your distant relatives, all weird uncles and aunts you never see apart from when there's a family wedding. No worries about having closer family over at yours and feeling awkward because they'll expect you to play a tune on the fiddle because it's Christmas even though they couldn't give a shit the rest of the year, or about who's going to get pissed and need looking after, or if you get left alone with your little cousins and are expected to babysit them while they cry because they're over-wrought and want to go to bed. It must be nice to just get back to basics, perhaps have a nice dinner and just spend time together with your family and being thankful for just having them without all that guff.

Ellyn holds the dress down on the floor for me to step into.

It's heavy as she slides it over my arms. It's also tight, as she does me up at the back. I feel something crick as she pulls tight on the ribbons.

'Is he out for a laugh, this bloke, or what?' I thought it was meant to be the Victorians who invented clothes that meant you couldn't breathe but were all hunky dory as long as they appealed to the menfolk, because you always had to bow down to poxy men, health risk or not.

Ellyn laughs.

'Oh, but Benevolence looked a vision in this gown. Methinks you shall show her up to look a hag by comparison!'

Is she bloody kidding me or what? The sick bastard's gone and picked the dead woman's dress for me to wear? That just doesn't seem kosher. I itch all over, all of a sudden, and it's not just because the velvet is too hot for the May Day sun.

'So, is there a headdress or a hat or what that matches this?' I say, itching my arms.

'None,' Ellyn says, then comes at me with a wooden comb. She leads me gently to the little window seat. 'Although we are to make you appear as much like her as may be possible.'

I think back to the portrait of Lady Benevolence in Donald's place as Ellyn attacks my head. I've not put a brush through it since I've been here, so it's hardly surprising that it canes as she combs. Benevolence's portrait showed her in green, like me – check. Loose hair hanging down – check, as soon as Ellyn's done. But I'm still not going to look like a thirty- or forty-something woman, no matter how much dolling up I get. I'll still look like a scruffy college girl, whatever fancy gear I put on. The thought *chokes* me up a bit – I shouldn't be getting

193

ready to marry and die, I should be doing things that girls my age do. That's going to classes, thinking about the future and having fun with Matty, playing our music and having a crack.

'That will have to suffice,' Ellyn says, placing the comb down next to me. I can just about make half of my reflection out in the glass of the window. It's scary. I could almost pass for some medieval noblewoman. Maybe that's something to do with the spell. The *ritual*, this thing that's about to happen.

I can hear the faint strains of what sounds like chamber music coming from above me. It's beautiful, but it's sinister. I just know it means that wheels are about to spin.

Sure enough, a few minutes later, Thacks appears in the doorway. He's creepy as ever in a long black robe that makes him look like a druid. Apt, really, given the circumstances.

His face has no expression as he holds a hand out towards the door, beckoning me to follow.

"Tis time.'

28
Matty

We're riding on horseback, back to the woods. I'm sitting behind Lankin on top of one that's killing my legs and seems to be desperate to get me off by the way it's chucking me about, and Sarah-Jane and Allison are sharing the other. It pisses me off that nobody seems to be struggling to ride like I am. I don't even know where the animals came from – Sarah-Jane said that Allison had "acquired" them for us. Mysterious, indeed. More than likely they've been nicked from somewhere in the village.

'So, did you kill the prick in the end?' I holler to Sarah-Jane, though the wind and the thunder of hooves is against me.

'Come again?'

'William – you said you were going to kill him, didn't you?'

She grins, and that's only partly Allison's doing, who tightens her grip around Sarah-Jane's waist and leans into her.

'Aye, I fear I almost did. I did rain blows upon him before Allison returned my senses to me and bade we go after you. Yet he still had breath in him when we left,' she says, ducking to avoid a low branch. And then she falls quiet, and I think

I can just about hear Allison telling her not to think about him because even though they were to be married it's obvious that he cares not a jot for her now. She had better concentrate her energies on searching for one who will love her true, and kindly, treat her with as much respect and hold her in higher regard than even a queen. Seriously, why don't they just get it over with? It's so *obvious*.

The woods get denser as we ride, thicker and we need to do more ducking and dodging than when you're up against the gym wankers in dodgeball in P.E. This is a bit more painless, though.

'You sure this is the right way to this guy, you know?' I ask the middle of Lankin's back. Christ, he's so huge, I can't even hold on to him properly – I just have to hook my fingers in his belt and hope.

'Aye – he frequents where few dare to tread,' he says. 'Fear not, for we will shortly arrive.'

We ride for a few more minutes until it gets so thick that the horses can't get through. It's almost like a wall of tangled trees and bushes and brambles, and it's so dark – barely any light can come through. No wonder people don't dare to tread here, it's downright *weird*. We leave the horses where they are – for they will surely find their way back, Allison promises, although I feel a bit guilty for leaving them – and start through a tiny gap. Lankin leads, and at first it looks like he's going to get stuck because he's too big for the opening. Somehow, though, he makes it through, with the girls just behind and me last of all – though I wish I was in the middle, because it feels like there's something following me. There's not, as I see every time I glance backwards, but it's still not great to feel.

We break through the natural wall a minute or two later, and I'm completely stunned by what's waiting for us. There's a big old clearing edged by trees making a perfect circle. Sunlight bathes the entire scene, filtering through in lines. A river zig-zags through at an angle, and the water is so clear that even from here you can see the fish swimming and the underwater plant life swaying gently. On our side of the river, there are flowers in colours spanning the entire spectrum, and toadstools big enough to sit on. There's a sort of magic about this place, and there are tiny coloured specks in the air twinkling in the light, which disappear as soon as they came. I realise I'm holding my breath and exhale quickly.

The other bank more or less mirrors this one for vibrant natural stuff, only there's added animals, and also a man, sitting casually with his bare feet in the river. He's plucking idly at a small harp as a deer stands next to him, watching with intrigue, like it's the most wonderful thing it's ever seen. More than likely it's shocked by the big floppy hat he's wearing, red velvet with a huge green feather poking out, to match the red-and-green ensemble he's got on. He's essentially a living Christmas tree.

'Ho, Thomas!' Lankin calls, and the deer scarpers. The guy waves, and we find ourselves walking over to him, while I wonder why it's all right for every other sod to use "ho" as a greeting, but when I tried it I copped stick off Allison.

'*The sun doth cast its gold rays fair, 'pon this – not a man, for he's more like a bear!*' The man exclaims and wades through the water to get to us. He throws down his harp and hugs Lankin

197

without even a hello, and Lankin does the same – he really is like a bear, like the guy observed.

'You continue to write your silly poems, Thomas?' Lankin says, when they're done.

'I fear so, Lankin. 'Tis a pleasure to see you again, dear friend.'

I put two and two together, because I've twigged he's another character we've sung about.

'Don't tell me,' I say. 'You're the Thomas the Rhymer, aren't you?'

The guy takes his hat off, and bows before me, letting all his long hair tumble about his face like a shampoo advert.

'The very same! How come you by knowledge of my humble work?'

'It's a long story, mate,' I say, genuinely gutted because he's probably one of the few people here who'd appreciate what it is Sandy and I actually do.

'We have not the time, Matty,' Allison warns.

'Ah, now that is pity itself,' he says, putting his hat back on. 'Methought there would be some poetry to be had by your tale.'

'There probably is, and hopefully I can tell you all about it another time. But Lankin said you might be able to help us.'

He nods.

'Lankin and his friend have enabled the concealment of this, my special place, for some time now. I am indebted to him.'

Lankin clears his throat, and starts scratching at his beard, apparently embarrassed about coming outright with what he's about to ask.

'I understand that what I request of you is great, Thomas. Yet I rather hope that your lady might lend us her horse.'

No sodding way. We just got rid of two.

'*Another* horse? We seriously came all this way for another horse. You really are all shot!'

'I know not what "shot" means, but that would sound ungrateful,' Sarah-Jane hisses.

Lankin shakes his head.

'It matters not, Sarah-Jane. 'Tis not a regular filly, this horse we seek. Thomas?'

He nods and picks up his harp. It's a really lovely looking instrument, and I'd love to have a go on it. I bet it's like a Gibson for chamber musicians. He plays a little melody, a nice-sounding thing that makes you think you should be dancing with a troll in a forgotten underground kingdom, or else doing LARP at someone's wedding. It is magical music, quite complicated as I watch his fingers, until he ends it on a deafening minor note that makes me cringe because minor is always creepy. It rings out around the clearing. On the opposite bank, the trees begin to shake. At first, I think it must be a load of horses galloping towards us making the ground rumble, and that the tune is something Thomas does to summon them, like a farmer with a whistle.

It's not, though. The trees shake out of control, and out of place. They slide along the ground in two directions, opening up a path to some distant meadow, all hills and brilliant weather. Only it's pure white and sparkling, as though somebody's chucked a shedload of diamonds in that direction.

The twinkling colours of our clearing twinkle quicker and quicker, apparently mimicking my heartbeat, and the sound of thundering hooves. It really is beautiful, and I can hear everyone gasp. Including me.

Allison's voice cracks as she speaks.

'I have seen this road only in the visions conjured by the tales of troubadours and madmen. 'Tis the road to fair Elfland itself!'

Of course it is. Like anything surprises me anymore. But I feel my mouth go slack as the source of the thundering makes itself known in the vision. It's a horse, entirely silver, and riding it is the most beautiful woman I've ever seen that's not Sandy. She's stark bollock naked, except for a ghost of a cloak that seems to be actually made of light. It billows around her, and it gives her skin a paranormal sheen. The dinky white tiara she's got on seems real, though. She seems stuck, not getting any nearer despite riding at full pelt, and the noise of the hooves getting louder and louder.

And then, quickly as it came, it's gone. Everything's silent, and the path's disappeared. The trees look like they've never moved.

'Did it go wrong or something?' I ask nobody in particular.

And then I'm on my arse, I'm knocked flying backwards as the horse and rider stampede through thin air and clip me in the process; appearing out of thin air, like she's teleported herself out of that vision, with no warning or ceremony or anything. The woman pulls the horse to a halt before she can do a hit and run on my mates, stopping centimetres from Allison who's not had the sense to dive like the others. The witch doesn't even flinch, just stands staring with eyes glazed over like shop workers when they see the people working the next shift come in. This is obviously a big deal.

'That's what you call horsepower!' I say as I get up, to try and break the ice. It doesn't work, though, as nobody acknowledges me at all. They're all too into this bird and her horse. She slips off the grand beast – because that's the only way to describe him – and strokes his nose as Thomas rushes over to give her a cuddle. It's sweet, he lifts her up and they spin like in an old lovey-dovey film. I can just make out the pointed ears under her hair as it flies out around her. And then she steps forward, arms extended regally, to take Lankin's hands and squeeze them.

'Dear Lankin.' Her voice is odd, hushed like a whisper; and at the same time, it seems to echo around the clearing, tearing through the trees and buzzing through the ground. Sort of like the voice of God, if he turned out to be real, and he was actually a tasty, classy naked bird.

'Your majesty,' Lankin says, bending down on one knee like a knight. I go to do the same, thinking that it's the done thing, what you have to do in front of Elven royalty. Before my knee even touches the ground, I feel Allison yanking me up by my t-shirt. We watch as the Elf Queen takes Lankin's massive head in her ghostly hands and kiss his forehead.

'That which you seek is the very least we might do for you, my friend,' she says. 'You, who brought Thomas to me, and filled our once-empty lives with naught but love. We are indebted to you.'

She hasn't even asked what he wants; I realise. But I guess

either Thomas has communicated that to her in that melody he played, or else she's telepathic. Can elves be telepathic? God knows, but I'm not about to interrupt her flow.

The Elf Queen motions for Lankin to stand, and he does. And now she turns to me.

'Dear Matty,' she starts. It's definitely mind-reading, because not once have I been mentioned. 'Your quest is noble, and your heart, though you see it not, is pure. I will get you to Sandy in time.'

I feel my eyes tear up again. She's just so beautiful, and they're all so willing to help, these people. I really don't deserve it. I don't have words, and she doesn't even mind. She only smiles and whistles. Thundering through the ether come four horses, identical to hers.

'They will find their way back,' she says to all of us, sensing our collective concern that this is way too big a present to have off a mythical queen. 'You need only think of your destination, and they will bypass the human-trod path. They know the way. So mount, my friends, and think upon Dover. May you find that which you seek – and your journey's end, too!'

29

Sandy

I follow Thacks in silence down several corridors, with no sound but the rustling of this bloody gown and that chamber music, getting louder and louder the further into the castle we go. I expect us to be let out into some grand hall, perhaps the keep, where all the servants will be waiting in lines for our approach. Instead, we head up one of the spiral staircases – in one of the towers, as I remember from the layout of other castles I've been to at home. He moves quickly for an old boy, or perhaps I'm just slowed up by the restricting dress – I have to hold it up to keep from tripping and feel like a real tit as I realise my breathing's getting quicker as I can't take deep breaths to keep me going.

We end up on the actual top of the castle – I'm screwed if I know whether that's for dramatic effect or ritualistic purposes, but it's certainly different. It's almost beautiful. The sun is still high in the sky, but there's a breeze coming off the sea that keeps me from starting to sweat, even in the dress, even in front of all Donald's people. They're standing to attention and turn to stare at us, even though nobody announces us. I wonder if that's another of Thacks's little tricks.

'My lady,' someone behind me says, and grabs my arm.

'William? I thought you were looking after Donald's place? I never saw you leave with us.'

'Aye,' he says, and I can't help but look at his actual eye, which is shiny and puffed right out since the last time I saw him. I want to laugh, because it looks hilarious on his tiny thin face. 'There was a change of circumstances, and so comes it I find myself... *able* to attend.'

Something in his tone tells me he was forced to come and got here by magic. Of course. He leads me through the middle of the people – *down the aisle* and I would be sick if it wasn't for this bloody dress. I could still run, could yank myself away from William and at least try, even if I know there is no escaping this. I'd even launch myself into the sea, a whole castle and cliff below, if we were only a little less inland, and I'm really not keen on heights. Even extreme tombstoning would be less scary than what's happening now.

I'm shocked even more when William puts his other hand on mine and squeezes it – I hadn't noticed until then that I'm shaking. His fingers are long and cold, but I'm grateful. He shoots me a look that tells me not to worry, not really – but then, what does he know about weddings? He ran away from his own, after all. He deserves that black eye, just for that – but then, nobody's all bad, as his tiny gesture's surely shown.

The aisle's only about ten people deep but has seemed to go on for a while. His pace is slower than I was expecting – is he stalling for me? Awaiting us – awaiting me – up the front, is Donald, looking harsh all in black, but smiling, and a priest. Or

I think he's a priest. He looks all official, in robes, and he's got a book in front of him – *the* book, I notice, or a version of it – and a load of ribbon in one hand. It's quite a pretty set-up too – there's a wooden arch, covered in flowers, and a table with a white cloth. I shiver, though, as I cop a sight of something just behind the priestly guy – it's a box, but a very specific wooden box with gold handles, just twinkling in the sun to catch my eye.

Benevolence Donald is here, and pretty soon I won't be. I swallow hard, wondering if they'll put me in the same coffin when they're finished, and for some reason that makes my eyes prickle. It's either the thought of that, or the whimpering of Matty Dog I can hear from somewhere in the back that makes me wonder if I'll ever get to fuss him, or Ozzy, again. He's somehow managed to follow us up from the chamber. I turn to look at him, and see he's being held by one of the servants, crouched down and hands at his neck, holding him steady – it's Mercy, I think, going by the dress. It's hard to tell in the sun.

William leaves me next to Donald. I feel him grasp my hand, tight like he wants to break it off. I get that he's excited and wanting to get on with the whole thing, but that's so unnecessary. I let my own fingers stay limp.

The priestly guy holds his hands up, and the band shuts up. This would be the time the congregation would sit down, if there were any seats. I don't look at Donald, or at Thacks – I don't dare, because one word or look from either of them will make me do something mental. I can't cause a scene, because that'll only speed the process up, and I need all the time I can get in case Matty can make it. It's hopeless, but the thought of just seeing his cheeky bastard face again will make all of this bearable.

Priestly guy shrieks something in what sounds like a foreign language, and I just about shit the dress right up. It takes a while to register that it's Old English, the pre-Chaucer kind that not even academics can decipher sometimes. Blow that.

Donald seems to follow the gist of it, not taking his eyes off the bloke. Mine, though, keep wandering to the coffin behind him. I never even got this close to my great gran's coffin after she hoofed it. I was only at her funeral under duress, too. Donald squeezes my hand again, bringing me back to earth, and I see the priestly guy staring at me.

'Brád?' He asks me in his weirdo language.

I shrug.

'Brad? What d'you mean?'

'He requires your hand, my dear,' Donald says.

'Oh, right.' Donald's still holding my right hand tight, so I stick my left fist out. He takes it, puts Donald's right one on top, and starts wrapping the ribbons around them, tying us together. A handfasting.

'Now, if it pleases you to mirror my words. We commence with the Lord Donald,' the priest says, finally in proper words.

Two times we hear it – first from him, and then from Donald.

'I Donald take thee Sandy to be my wedded wife, to have and to hold from this day forward, for better for worse, for richer for poorer, in sickness and in health, till death us depart, if Jove will it ordain, and thereto I plight my trough.'

Now, it's real. It sounds like a proper wedding, and I wish the castle would just swallow me up into its walls. It's my turn now, and I wonder if there'll be repercussions if I balls it up. There seem an awful lot of words to remember as the priestly guy gives them for me to repeat.

'I Sandy take thee Donald to be my wedded husband, to have and to hold from this day forward, for better for worse, for richer for poorer, in sickness and in health, to be bonoure and buxum in bed and at board –'

'Ease up, mate,' I say, jarring a bit. I nod towards Donald. '*He* didn't have to say that bollocks about being buxom in bloody bed!'

Thacks scoffs and snatches the book up from in front of us.

'They are but words, Sandy. So happens that you need not take pains to carry out their meaning.'

Even though he's got a point, it's still bollocks and I'm not having it.

'Plenty of girls here do, though, and that's not on. Screw your double standards,' I say, and spit straight at him. I don't know where it comes from, it just seems the right thing to do. His milky eye twitches, and he opens the book.

'Sire, we must press on if we are to complete the ritual in time,' he says through gritted teeth. Donald's stunned by my display, it seems. Hesitant almost – it strikes me that he might not actually want to do this, even if it is his missus they're wanting to resurrect. He swallows and shuts his eyes as he tells me:

'Sandy, please – if you will only say the words and bring this to an end, we need not extend your suffering.'

I think I've suffered enough, though I don't tell him that. I only finish the bollocks words, just to get it over with – because, really, he's right for once. Why hang it out? Why put off the inevitable? I've never been a procrastinator, and I'm not about to start this close to death.

The priest starts to tie a bow with the ribbons binding mine and Donald's hands, but he stops short.

'Wherefore stoppest you, sir? Come along,' says Donald.

'Please, sire,' he says, looking behind us, 'methinks something is afoot.'

I turn to look – the last few rows of the congregation have deserted the ranks, gathering at the far end of the roof and craning their necks over the parapet. I can just make out a few concerned remarks.

'Be it an attack?'

'Nay, there's a woman on one of them.'

'Such beautiful creatures!'

One thing Donald and I seem to agree on is that something's not right. Hands still tied, we both take legs to see what's occurring.

'Let us pass!' Donald thunders, forcing his way through the people. My knee knocks against the stone and makes me buckle. I grab Donald's arm for support, and he's stiff as a corpse.

I squint at the four figures everyone's talking about, and it's like I've seen a ghost. There's a woman with a great billowing cloak and mad hair, and three guys, riding horses that shine like silver in the sun. This one guy at the end looks a bit like Matty.

Then William mutters under his breath, but it's right in my earhole.

'Confound it, Sarah-Jane.'

I know it. It's Matty, and he's actually *here*.

30
Matty

The Elf Queen's right, it's as simple as thinking about where you need to get to once you're on the horse. Getting on the horse is probably the hardest bit, especially as there's no saddle or anything, and it's not something I'm in the habit of doing. I just hold on, grabbing onto his mane tight and squeezing my legs tight against him, and hope like mad that I don't fall off. I picture Dover Castle in my mind, shutting my eyes to shut out the meadow, and the guys, and to get it clear. It could almost be a postcard image I think of. All at once, I feel my horse rear up and whinny before running ahead at full pelt, and I feel a shock in both shoulders. The wind stings, and my eyes stream, and I feel like a pisshead on holiday on a bucking bronco ride. I tighten my grip as I hear Sarah-Jane do a real Thorpe Park shriek through the whooshing in my ears.

'Matty, behold!'

'I'd rather not,' I holler back, knowing that if I do, then the force might rip my eyes right out of their sockets, stringy bits and all.

'Nay, but you must open your eyes! You want to miss this

not!'

She's probably right, because it's not every day you get to ride a mythical queen's royal horse. Against my better judgement, I force my eyes open – and through the tears, it's like the Tardis on LSD. We're riding through something sure enough, but there's no ground for the horses' hooves to pound. We're riding through nothing but light, the entire bloody spectrum spinning around us like a hippie's nightmare.

'This is mental!' I holler, and I want to scream but I clock something ahead. It's a pinhole of pure white light, gradually opening up wide, and all too soon the fantastic light is history. Now, I can feel the sun on me and the sting of the salty breeze as we gallop on actual ground – the cliff tops of Dover. Straight ahead is the castle, and I feel my guts leap up as I clock a group of people crowding up at the top, hanging over like vultures as we approach.

I don't like the way they're craning over. Are they gawping at us? Is it because we're in time to ruin the whole set-up and save Sandy? That they're shitting themselves because the rescue team is actually here? Or is it the complete opposite – that we're too late after all and they've come to crow, and point and stare? Whatever. We're here quicker than I ever thought possible, and the horses are flooring it.

'Take up your sword!' Sarah-Jane bellows, even though we've a few hundred feet of run-up left. I reach under for it, wedged dodgily between my leg and the horse's side for not-so-safekeeping.

'Don't tell me we still have to fight these knobends?' I say.

Allison cackles.

211

'Come, Matty! Thought you it would be so simple as to walk in and take Sandy in your arms, as a hero of antiquity might?'

Well, actually, yeah, I don't tell her. Guess I didn't really think this far ahead about what would happen once we got here.

Lankin hollers at the rear of us. I can't believe he's still with us for this leg of the journey, either, though he's got his own bone to pick with Donald when we get there. I force myself to look left, to see what he's shouting about. The Downs are covered in animals of all sizes, headed towards us and to the castle. Towering over them is Jack-in-the-Green, wading through the carpet of creatures towards us.

'You would join us in this fight?' Lankin asks as soon as Jack's in earshot.

'Did I not say I hoped Matty would find his ladylove? Thought you I had forgotten about this quest? I did leave you to ensure the safety of my creatures, but so comes it they had thought to track you to the Elven glade and reported your intentions to me. Now, let us all be engaged in this!'

I notice Allison's wand come out, but she only waves it in Jack's direction. Immediately his brown bits become a bit less brown, and his movements are more fluid as he strides alongside us. A witchy power-up, perhaps.

'I suppose you are a good bush, in your way,' Allison says. 'Thank you.'

He seems to blush at that – at least that's what I guess is the case when spirits of nature suddenly sprout pink flowers all over. They're blown off by the wind soon enough.

I have to give up holding the horse's mane with my one sword-less hand – the wind is threatening to rip it out of my grip, and even now, with two hands, it's still fighting to be free. The castle walls loom up ahead, squirrels scaling right up them and the less mobile animals creating a hubbub around the bottom. There's no sign of any other life at ground level, yet the horses slow without our say-so. The drawbridge we went through only yesterday is still down, and as we approach, there's no sign of anybody manning the gatehouse. It's really not the best example for running a bloody fortification.

I get off my horse and run forward, sword out in front of me – ready to bash any bastard that comes near, if they ever do. It's all a bit like *déjà vu* – I'm expecting Dimsby and his lot to come out and attack us again at any minute. Instead, it's completely still, and we make it through the bailey quickly without any aggro this time. Everyone left the horses the other side of the gatehouse, and looking back I see they're happy enough, probably getting ready to "make their own way back" to the Elf Queen, as she'd put it.

'I can hear *music*,' Lankin says, stunned.

'Aye. We need to get to the top of this place,' Sarah-Jane says. 'Lest the unmentionable occur.'

With that, Sarah-Jane and Lankin speed off to the entranceway. They hang back a bit, like military personnel checking it all out before "going in".

'Take care,' Allison hisses, pointing her wand straight up. Her face is creased up in anguish like she knows something's up, and I wonder if she's got a radar spell that lets you know when people are coming your way. It'd explain how she knew I was on my way to her tower when we first met. Funny how all the little things start to make sense after a while.

Sarah-Jane nods and keeps her sword up. I feel sorry for Lankin with just his knife, which is dinky in comparison. All those sharp things at his gaff, you'd have taken something a bit meatier on a day out, surely?

Something zooms out of the door, whacking straight into Lankin and sending him arse over tit. At first, I think it's a bloke in a grey cloak, bent over like something in a horror film, but Sarah-Jane sheathes her sword and starts putting her hands all over the thing.

'The hell is *that*?' I shout, because it's more than big enough to have her hands off and God knows what it's doing to Lankin's face at the minute.

"Tis a *dog*, Matty!' Sarah-Jane squeals. The dog stops attacking Lankin's face and cocks his slobber-smothered head, like it's his name she's just said.

'No way! Are you Matty Groves? The *other* one?' I say.

The dog barks, and Lankin's looking like he wants to cry the biggest man tears ever as he sits on the floor hugging the grey beast to him, so it can only be him. The dog Matty nuzzles into Lankin's chest, giving off little excitement whimpers. Perhaps this Donald isn't such a murderous bastard, all things considered. Still, we've got to get a lick on in case that's not true.

'Listen… *Matty*,' I say, hesitating because saying your own name is weird even if it is a different person you're talking to. 'If you understand me, then please help me. Is Sandy here?'

There's another affirmative-sounding bark, and he wriggles

free of Lankin's bear hug to run back inside. He pauses in the doorway, wanting us to follow by the look of it, and as soon as we move towards him he bolts off down the corridor.

We don't get very far before the dog bounds into a little side room. I decide to ignore it, seeing as he's a dog and must still get distracted by doggy kinds of things, and go to run straight past. I stop in my tracks when I hear a voice that I recognise, even if it is muffled.

'Groves!'

We go in after the dog, and he's circling two men, all tied up on the floor. It's Henry, gagged with a scarf, and Spuds – *Dimsby* – tied back-to-back on the floor like some medieval bondage scenario gone wrong and left to be forgotten about.

Lankin cuts through the ropes in record time to let them free, and to my surprise Henry hugs me close.

'What happened?' I ask, struggling to breathe as his kingly death-cuddle squashes my lungs up inside me.

'Dear friends! You have not much time – your maiden still breathes, even now,' Henry says. He cocks his head, listening to the faint strains of music. 'Aye, take the stairs past the hall where first we met. May Jove go with thee. Come, Dimsby.'

He tears himself away, grabs Dimsby and flies past the girls.

'Oi, but where are you going?' I holler.

'Wait and see – I shall catch thee up!'

And quick as that, the king and his man are gone. We don't see their arses for dust. The dog cocks his leg by the door and then shoots off again with the wind up his flue. We twist and turn down corridors, just trusting the new Matty, and finally we reach the stairs.

'I like this not,' Sarah-Jane says, echoing what we're all thinking as we start up the winding staircase. 'We have yet to encounter any of Donald's band. 'Tis as though the castle were *abandoned*.'

Only it's not, because the music's getting louder the higher we go. It's a quick way up, but that's only because I'm taking two at a time despite the burning in my thighs.

It's dark, the only light coming in through the odd couple of glassless windows, and more than a few times I stumble, having to put my arms out, sword and all, to try and get my balance back. Nearer the top, there's more light, and the dog creeps up instead of bounding up like he has been. I overtake him on the stairs, and rather than taking it slower in case Donald or his henchman's waiting to spear me through, I run right out through the archway and onto the roof.

There's a crowd, but not a huge one. They're all still hanging over the side or fighting off all the woodland creatures and birds that have made their way up here and started a sneak attack. And over on the other side, I see her. She's there, and she's *alive*.

'Sand!'

31

Sandy

I look up as I hear someone shout my name from the tower we'd come up by. It's a guy in a t-shirt and jeans, and he looks like he's got a sword. Bloody hell it's him, it's really Matty and I want to scream and cry and laugh, but instead I continue trying to rip myself away from William's grip. I can't believe Thacks and his instructions to William to lock me up for safekeeping. I'm not a bloody necklace or wad of twenties you want to keep plugged up somewhere.

'Come, my dear,' he says, putting his other hand on my waist and trying to lead me away, towards the seaward tower. 'You need not watch.'

'Never mind watch, I've got to bloody do something!'

So I do, and I crunch his toes with my foot. He lets go of my waist but still has me by the wrist, so with my free hand I thrust the palm up against his already bruised nose, which makes him cry out and let go.

I don't tell him sorry, but instead run straight for Matty because he's a stupid sod for coming here, but he's my stupid sod and I'm ecstatic to see him and his stupid face. I dodge the chaos of animals and people struggling against each other, squirrels trying to scratch eyes out and birds flapping their wings by way of distraction, and people trying to brush insects off them, and launch myself at him, kind of meeting him halfway as he sprints to me, too.

'You're alive!' He says, giving me the biggest cuddle I think I've ever known him give. His arms are familiar, and I feel myself tearing up.

'Just! Cut that one a bit fine, didn't you?' I say.

He jerks back like he's going to go on the defensive, but he just starts laughing when he clocks my face and sees that it's a joke. I swear I see him wipe away a tear as well, and I wonder what's happened to him. He didn't even cry at the notebook fiasco at college.

'Where is the prick?' Matty says, business-like and sniffing like he's wanting to hide the relief.

'Which one?'

'I do believe I be the "prick" he refers to,' Donald says, behind me. We both turn to look as he plucks a squirrel from his shoulder and sets it down on the ground. It scurries off without a second glance.

'I must commend you for your efforts, boy. To find your ladylove, you would keep the company of witches and murderers and... Jove knows what *that* may be,' he says, wrinkling his nose at something that's just rolled over the parapet. It looks like a living tree, and it shoves two branches out from its sides. Immediately, all the animals abandon their fight with Donald's servants and run to its branches, or else head straight over the parapet ready for the vertical climb back down. Likewise, half of Donald's staff leg it at the sight of the weird tree man. The other half leg it as a ridiculously big ghost squeezes itself through the doorway to the tower, some even launching themselves over the side with fright. Whatever, I'm used to the shocks by now, and it's when King Henry and his man appear from behind her looking really pleased with themselves that I know everything's sweet. He even winks at Matty.

'Of course, I'd keep that company,' Matty says, proud. 'These are my *friends.*' I have a quick look at his gang behind us, and work out who must be Sarah-Jane Taylor, brandishing a wicked-looking sword, and the witch in her witchy garb, though I'm not sure who the mountain man is. I only know I could kiss every single one of them all for helping Matty, and it's all for me and they don't even know me. I don't deserve any of this.

'Thackeray,' Donald coos, clapping his hands. 'See and deal with this wraggle-taggle party. We must press on.'

And all at once Thacks is there with his milky eye and his smug pissing face, and his hand clenching and unclenching around something. It can't be good.

'Allison Gross,' he says, with the smallest hint of surprise. 'Methought I had seen the last of thee.'

The witch grins, wand in hand. It quivers quietly – dangerously. It's the quiver of rage but wanting to keep your shit together.

'Aye, I might say the same of thee. Perchance you thought yourself cunning, to cast a spell on the people of Kent? To infect the mind of the populace so that they thought your teacher were naught but a wicked old witch, and not the healer she did originally seek to be?'

I hear Matty mutter, 'no way' and even Sarah-Jane and the mountain man seem to bristle. These two must go way back.

Her voice is a whisper now.

'I was respected, Thackeray. Revered, one might say. You stripped all that from me, forcing me to live the rest of my existence alone in that accursed tower. You robbed me of my life. I shall be damned to the eternal fire if I would let thee do the same to my friends!'

Then with a mad howl that makes my innards vibrate, she storms forward and starts lashing electricity at Thacks. It shoots out in every colour under the sun, cracking, thundering and shaking the castle. The old boy has to move quick to dodge and shoot red thunderbolts back, straight from his fingers. Allison manages to deflect them all, sending them straight back his way. It's a good job all his servants have scarpered because there'd be more than a few casualties with the way this magic's flying about.

'You two were better gone from this place while you still have breath within you,' the mountain man says to Matty, and tries to usher us away.

'No, I'm staying. You've done the same for me – for *us*,' he says, and looks at me like he wants my blessing. He doesn't even need to ask, though Christ knows what good we're going to do.

I nod and look for Donald. He's standing with his mouth agape, watching the magic people hurling attacks at each other like he's watching the pay-per-view death match on the telly.

Behind him, William and Sarah-Jane are having their own set-to, oblivious of what's going on around them. William's managed to nab a sword from somewhere, and they're fighting it out and spitting insults. I just twig Sarah-Jane cast a glance at the sorcerers' battle before ending it all with a swift punch to the stomach, which doubles him over. One more up the throat sends William to the ground, knocked sparko. Allison's on all fours now, sweating and panting like she's going to hyperventilate.

'Ástierf!' Thacks bellows, and thrusts both hands out. They glow a macabre red that gets more and more intense. This isn't good.

'Allison – hold!'

And as she shouts, Sarah-Jane sprints across, throwing herself in front of the witch and into the path of Thackeray's burning ball of death.

32
Matty

Sarah-Jane bears the full brunt of Thackeray's magic. She yells as it knocks her flying back into Allison, taking the pair of them over. She does a kind of backwards roll and finally crumples into a limp heap on the floor.

It's not right. So much life to be snuffed, just like that. I feel like I want to chuck up, and even Thackeray looks stunned by her grand gesture. As for Allison, once she's twigged what's happened she chucks down the wand and starts bawling. I hug Sandy close as her inhuman cries rip through all of us.

'There'll be no more of this *idiocy*,' Donald says. His voice, I notice, seems to waver. 'Thackeray, complete the ritual.'

'Sire, the marriage is not yet complete,' he says. 'I fear —'

'*I* fear you understand not. Our hands were bound, were they not? This should do well enough. Complete the ritual.'

'Sire,' Thackeray concedes, and turns on his heel, over to what looks like an altar on the other side of the roof.

'Hold on a minute, no! No, I won't let you, not now I've come all this way. Like it makes a difference anyway — I'll do whatever it takes to save Sand, and my friends.'

I feel the sword in my hand – still there, still cold. It's comforting, like I've still got Sarah-Jane backing me up, and not lying still on the ground. Nobody's taking a blind bit of notice of me. It's like my words aren't even registering, like they don't matter. They're just words, after all, and I've got to act. It's what *she* would do.

'Don't let him get the book!' Sandy gasps and starts running before I get a chance to take legs myself. I know it. It just has to be *the* book, same as the one that brought us here, and I'll be buggered if we're having any more of that aggro.

It happens too fast to even register, but the dog, out of nowhere, leaps up and latches onto Thackeray's arm. He keeps him there for a few seconds as he tries to shake him off, just long enough for Allison to get to her feet, face still dripping with tears, and to cast something right at him.

'Ástierf thyself!' She cries, and a sheet of red light pummels down on Thackeray and shoots right through him. I swear I see his skeleton shake, silhouetted in the crimson curtain. I nearly lose my balance with the earthquake it causes, and Sandy grabs my arm to keep us both from keeling over.

Allison falls to her knees before he does. She stays upright, though, unlike the old man who falls onto his front with a sickening crack, his eyes rolled up into his head. The dog barks, gruffly, and Lankin takes it upon himself to take the body up in his arms. He carries it over to the nearest parapet, and just drops it over the side, into the sea. Good riddance, and all that. You can almost feel the closure he must be feeling – it's one small victory in Elenore and Alys's memory. And who can blame him? It doesn't help Allison, though, who just keeps on crying silently.

'Fine!' Donald screams, his face redder than the magic. It's an expression I've not seen before – where he's been pretty subdued, his eyes are like two white holes now, and his teeth are bared like a rabid dog. It's scary, and I feel Sandy's grip on me tighten. This is wrong – she's had to live with this bloke, she can't have seen him like this either, going on how stiff she is.

He storms over to Sarah-Jane's body, and stoops, reaching for the sword still in her hand.

'No! Touch her not! Touch her *not*!' Allison claws at his elbow. He wriggles free of her hands and puts a foot into her chest to toe her away. The grip on my own sword tightens as he wrenches Sarah-Jane's out of her possession.

'I will not have my plan ruined at this, the last hour! Look you – May Day is almost over!' He points to the sun – it's hanging very low in the sky, now that he mentions it. He rushes to the book, lying flat against the white cloth of the makeshift altar, and shoots a look at us as he tries to find his chill.

'Sandy, come, and let us not prolong your suffering needlessly.'

I feel Sandy start to shake.

'You can jog right on!' She says, nearly laughing. 'You think I'm going to let you kill me now?'

'Play no games with me, Sandy,' Donald says. He keeps wetting his lips, like he's nervous and knows he's in danger of not getting his own way. 'We did explain it to you plain. You knew your blood was required to revive Benevolence.'

Just hearing the words set me on edge, and I have to do it. I tear myself away from Sandy and run at him.

'Require *this*, you bastard!'

But he blocks me, quick. Our swords clash so loudly that it feels like my eardrums might burst. He's strong for his age, and with a one-handed shove of his sword he forces me back, away from him and the altar. The book's still in his other hand, I notice, and there's got to be some way of getting it off him, even if we are busy playing swords. I don't get time to think, though, as he starts chucking all sorts of blows at me – overhead, spinning round for a sneaky one, and really hard ones that even send sparks flying. I shut my eyes for those, against my better judgement.

And all the while Sandy is screaming at us to stop, just stop the pair of us, but none of us bother to listen because we just keep on at it. All up my arms and my shoulders and even my back and legs are burning, and sweat is pouring off me. Even Donald's getting short of breath. Why won't anybody help us? Or maybe they are doing stuff I can't see because I'm concentrating on dodging and blocking, and suddenly I feel stone jar up the back of my legs. I feel myself going top heavy and nearly keel over the parapet. My arms go crazy trying to grab the stone, and, like a stupid prick, I drop the sword over the side behind me, into the sea. Donald pulls me back by the shirt and holds me close to his face, and I see the hairs of his moustache part as he breathes, like a bull, through his nose.

'You *will* witness this, Groves. I let one Matty Groves get away with his life, perhaps the greatest mistake I ever made besides confiding in Thackeray. But you – I want you to suffer as *I* have suffered,' he hisses at me. I feel his grip loosen ever so slightly and take the chance to knee the book straight out from under his arm. He lets go with a gasp, and scrambles to grab it from off the floor, but I boot it across to the dog. It hits a stone and somersaults, pages fluttering open, but he cops hold of the spine in his mouth and pads over to Lankin and Allison who are bent over Sarah-Jane's body.

I stumble over to the altar as Donald's mouth hangs in disbelief, thinking maybe I can jump him and hurl him over to meet the same fate as my sword. Instead, my stomach lurches as Sandy rushes towards me – with Donald and his sword, raised up over his head like a nutcase, close behind. She twists away from me, shoving one hand into my chest so I smack against the altar, and sticking the other one out in front of her in some dramatic superhero stance. She's trying to save me. She knows he won't do her in without the book.

'Sandy, step aside,' Donald says. His face has changed again, and now it's almost pleading. It's a bit worrying how quickly his mood changes.

'No chance,' she says, not moving an inch.

'Play no games with me, girl! We've not the time,' he says, grabbing her wrist. She wrenches it right out.

'Forget it, mate! If you're gonna kill him, you'll do me first – you might as well. That's the plan, right?'

'Sand, no!' I try to struggle out from under her hand. She's like lead and I can barely budge. I never knew she was so strong.

I hear Donald cry out. I see the blade. I see it go back over his head, two hands on the handle, and he brings it down with all his might. Sandy ducks her head and brings in her elbow to level her arm out as Donald slices it. There's blood, but she barely whimpers. She doesn't move, still locked in her superhero pose. Still *living*.

The blood drips from Donald's sword and from her wound, and it pools on the ground. It trickles through the grooves between the stones and appears to take on a life force of its own. It trickles towards something behind me. The coffin.

We all kind of watch, stunned, because I doubt any of us have ever seen blood move that way. It seems to thicken up on its journey too, and then veins upwards over the coffin, following the grain of the wood and actually wrapping itself around the gold handles. Then it collects itself together in a slimy red sheet and sucks itself into the crack between the lid and box, like an octopus I once saw escaping its tank. And now, there's silence.

Donald takes a step forward, sword still in hand, but he doesn't go for Sandy again. He takes another step towards the coffin. She takes the opportunity to rip off a bit of her dress and tries to tie it around her still bleeding arm with the other hand.

'Give us a hand? Do it tight,' she instructs, making a fist.

'We've got to find a doctor or something,' I say, making a dodgy knot. She doesn't even wince.

We just finish the field surgery when there's one solitary, loud knock. It can only be coming from one place, and I really don't want to look. Luckily Donald's bent over the coffin, hiding whatever's stirring under the lid.

'Did it work? You didn't need to kill me after all?' Sandy

227

says, full of it as ever despite the injury and the complete and utter bollocks that's happened today.

'Silence!' Donald hisses, pressing his ear to the lid. 'We needed only spill the blood of another Matty Groves' lady – no amount was specified. So, comes it Thackeray was convinced that we needed it all, lest the spell prove weak.'

I shouldn't, but I feel bad for the old sorcerer now – he only wanted to do a good job for his master, same as I only want to do right by my mates. Only I try not to hurt people to do it.

There's another knock, louder this time, and Donald backs away. Even the ghost in the tower screams and legs it back down the way she came, Henry and Dimsby in her wake. Seconds later, the wood lid of the coffin virtually explodes, splinters and slivers scattering everywhere. In the centre of the newly bored hole is a fist – a decomposed fist. It flexes its fingers, and grabs onto the side of the hole. Another hand appears on the other side, and I just see the top of a rotting head begin to peek out.

"Tis Benevolence, sure,' a weak voice near us croaks. I spin around, grateful to have a reason to tear my eyes away from the living dead – only to see more of the same. Sarah-Jane's eyes are open, and she's trying to sit up. Allison goes in for a hug before thinking better of hurting her more and rests her hands on her knees. She tells her not to move, and her eyes widen as she clocks the scene behind me. I turn back.

The half-rotted Benevolence is out of the coffin and starting to flesh out as Sandy's blood veins out all over her body. She looks more and more human as the muscles reform under her funeral dress, and skin begins to form, grey fading into colour, and hair sprouts from her bald head, falling about her shoulders. Her eyes come last, dropping into their sockets, and she raises her hands in front of her, as though her seeing is absolutely fine, but believing what's there is off the scale. Then she notices Donald, bent over on the floor as though somebody's socked him in the stomach, head bent down. She reaches for him, smiling, and lifts his head up. He clutches the hand at his cheek, sobbing his old bastard heart out.

'Why cry you, Donald?' Her voice is honey, and human, although it has a weird echo like you'd expect a ghost to have.

The bloke can't even speak, he just lurches forward and presses his head into her middle, hugging her legs like a child and still crying his eyes out. It's painful to watch, and I feel my guts twist up. She rests a hand on his head and looks at me and Sandy, and sighs.

'Why do you do this, Donald? Why do you take it 'pon yourself to torment – nay, to *torture* these young people so?'

Does this mean she's been watching in the afterlife or whatever comes once your time's up? Donald seems to think so, and grabs her wrist, kissing her hand like a desperate churchgoer kisses the priest that pardons them.

'I missed you,' he says, finally finding his voice. 'I needed you – I *still* need you!'

'But *this*,' she says, gesturing to her body, 'this is unnatural.'

'F-forgive me,' he says, bowing his head.

'I forgive the way Thackeray turned your mind. I forgive the way you took control of Kent, and even the way you seek to overthrow your own king Henry. *This* will not prove easy to forgive.'

'But I *love* you!'

'Then let love live on! Let this pair love each other and live!' She smiles at me and Sandy, and I don't know whether to bow or say thanks or what, so I kind of do both. Then she drops to her knees, so that she is level with Donald. 'You need not my body – you need only my *memory*. What good will the vessel do you if it be empty?'

'You understand not...' he says and then mumbles things that we can't hear.

'I think I understand enough. Please – let the young lovers be and let me rest. And above all else, *forgive*. You must forgive yourself, and forgive Lankin, and Matty. And you must forgive me – *please*. If you can do all this, I shall be at peace – and I shall always be with you.'

I think we're all about to burst out in tears, so I'm grateful when Henry and Dimsby return. There's a worrying cloud of smoke that puffs out from the tower behind them.

'Come!' He points to the opposite tower. 'The ghost has ushered everyone out of the castle – it is now our turn!'

'What's that?' I ask, pointing at the smoke.

'Yea, verily have I set the castle aflame.'

'*What?!* Why?' Sandy huffs, wiping her eyes.

'It did appear to be a good idea, at the time. To be rid of... all... *this*,' he says, waving his arm in the general direction of Benevolence and Donald, who are locking lips in one disturbing but touching farewell.

'Fair point.'

A throat clears behind me.

'If it please you, I know a quicker exit.'

I spin around, and it's William. He's got Sarah-Jane in his arms, and she's breathing, just. Allison and Lankin stand behind.

'We must seek out a barber-surgeon *immediately*.'

'What about Donald?' Sandy says, looking back.

'Let him stay,' I say, and grab her hand. 'At least they're together. He'll find his own way down if he wants to. But we need to hop it.'

She nods, and, following the dog, we all head into the tower, and leave Donald and Benevolence to it. I think they'll be all right. I *know* they'll be all right.

33
Matty

It's always quicker coming down than it is going up. We reach the ground in record time, quicker than it took me to hide from the police when I was nicking out of cars. We head a safe distance away from the burning castle, making the weirdest silhouette against an otherwise lovely sunset. May Day's nearly done and dusted, but we've still got to clue up a few things.

'You said you were a healer, witch – please, you have to save her. We'll not make a village in time,' William says, cradling Sarah-Jane's head in his lap. I guess he might really care, deep down. You'd have to, to marry someone – even just a little bit.

Allison puffs, her eyes brimming, and scratches her head with her wand.

'I-I've no spell that can remedy this.'

'But the spell – you used the same one on Thacks,' Sandy says, clapping her hands. 'Why did it kill him, but not her?'

'Aye, well the *galdor astiérf* will only kill those with no love within their hearts. If there is love, it will protect the heart and preserve the life within. The bodily injury will be great, mind you, and will eventually end the recipient. Unless...' she trails off her lesson, like she's just had her own eureka moment. Her eyes widen, and she clamps her hands on William's shoulders.

'You must kiss your wife, William Taylor!'

'Prithee?'

'That is all that may heal the wound – 'tis in my almanack! The only remedy that may cure the *galdor astiérf* is the kiss of true love.'

'A true love's kiss? What a load of old bollocks,' I huff, only to get elbowed by Sandy.

'Your efforts may be rewarded, William,' says Lankin. 'What harm be there to try?'

Sarah-Jane groans on the ground and looks paler than ever. He looks at her once before screwing up his eyes and bends double in an upside-down, fairy tale kiss. It's a perfect set-up – but she's still lying there, still as a statue.

'It worked not?'

There's a collective shake of heads. I see Sarah-Jane's lips move, ever so slightly. It looks like she's saying...

'Allison,' I say, nudging her. 'Perhaps you should have a crack at it.'

She choke-laughs and goes red as the sky.

'*I* should try? Be sensible, Matty.'

'Nah, seriously. Remember the fandom – remember your *ship*,' I say, wanting to squeal inside. Sandy's nose twitches like "what the hell are you on?" but I can explain it to her all later on when lives aren't at stake.

Allison sighs and tucks her hair behind her ears before sitting on the floor. She reaches over Sarah-Jane and kisses her full on the lips. My inner fanboy does somersaults as I see Sarah-Jane's hands reach up for Allison's head, and she sits up with all colour returning to her. And *still* they carry on.

Sandy starts clapping and *squee*-ing as much as I want to, because it's bloody cute, though the other blokes here don't really know what to do with themselves. They've probably never seen two women kiss like that in their lives, and they don't know whether to cry out in disgust or cheer them on. Instead, Henry clears his throat, and pats William on the back.

'You have proven yourself loyal, William, even if it has not quite, ah, been *reciprocated*,' he says, nodding at the girls. 'Should you seek new employment, I would gladly take you into my services.'

William gets to his feet and bows. 'Thank you, sire. Although if it be to your approval, I would sooner return to the Navy.'

'I do believe that can be arranged.' He smiles, and they shake hands. 'And what of you, Lankin?'

'You know who I am, sire?' Lankin says, flustered.

'I should think so! Donald spoke highly of you in my court before his mind clouded and he turned against me. Indeed, I do believe my men were sick to their garters from hearing about the seven-foot marvel who could dress gardens like no other. Methinks I could do with a gardener, when comes the time to build again,' he says, gesturing to his burning castle. 'What say you?'

'Aye!' He says, and grabs his hand, shaking it like he's pounding an invisible chocolate orange. 'Thank you, sire!'

'Nay, you must call me Henry. We must be on first-name

terms, must we not? Dimsby, introduce thyself.'

'I'm… well, Dimsby. I should look forward to working with you, Lankin.'

And just like that, the four blokes waltz off, discussing futures and planning all the great stuff that's going to come.

'And what now, Matty?' Allison asks, coming over with Sarah-Jane for one epic group hug with me and Sandy.

'What now? Shit! Yeah, *what* now?' I look at Sandy, my eyes are feeling like they're going to pop right out of my head.

'I don't know about you, but I'd really like to go home,' says Sandy.

'Obviously, but how do we do that?'

She gasps.

'Bugger! The *book*! We left it in the…' she trails off, and we all look at the castle in silence.

I clap my hands.

'No, wait. The dog had it, didn't he? On the roof… where's the dog?'

'*Matty* Dog had it?' says Sandy. 'Wait, where *is* Matty Dog?'

'Here, boy!' I holler, and start whistling like a loony.

'Come!' Sarah-Jane shouts, slapping her thighs.

And we all start shouting and whooping and whistling, but there's no sign of him. We start wandering back towards the castle, just in case he's been held up. I'm really hoping something bad hasn't happened to him.

Suddenly, Sandy stops.

'Matty – what if we're *stuck* here?'

'Do what?'

'What if we can't get back? I can't do this, I can't, it sucks here! I haven't had a bath, I reek to high heaven, I think I've got nits off one of the serving-girls from the estate, the food's shit, the clothes are shit, and if you're a girl, then you're bloody well screwed!'

'Whoa. Where's my nerd gone? I thought you liked all this "hey-nonny-nonny" stuff?'

'I thought I did. But the reality's shit, isn't it? People can change, you know.'

'I know.' I hug her tight, because I know this whole thing's changed me, too. 'There's got to be a way, I know it.'

'Ho!' Sarah-Jane calls us from near the edge of the cliff. She's holding something high, and as we get near, I see it's the book – battered and falling apart but looking whole. *Ish.*

'"Twould appear the text is complete,' affirms Allison.

'But where's Matty Dog? I-I was going to bring him home…' Sandy trails off, and hugs her stomach, head bowed.

I shake my head and grab her shoulder. 'Blow the dog – we've got the book, let's get out of here. He'll be all right.'

'Matty!' She shrugs off my hand, and crouches on the floor, face in her hands. *Shit*, we've got to find that dog before anybody thinks about going home. There's a beardy man I didn't notice before, standing on the cliff's edge, hands behind his back and just staring out at the sea. He could be one of Donald's lot, but doesn't seem very concerned about the burning castle if he is. Maybe he might have seen the dog.

'Excuse me, mate – you haven't seen a big grey dog hanging about, have you?'

He turns to look at me, and only smiles.

'Wherefore does Sandy cry?'

236

'How d'you know her name?'

'Think with your head. We Groveses are good at that.'

No way. He wanders over to Sandy, crouches.

'Sandy, grieve you not for me. Please.'

Her head snaps up like a child. One look in his eyes, and she launches herself on him, throwing her arms around him.

'Matty Dog! You're...!'

'Aye, is it not queer? When Thackeray died, it would appear his magic, too, came to an end. It did take its time, mind you – 'twas a powerful incantation.'

'You could still come with us, you know. I don't know if Mum would let you in the house in your current state, but...' She trails off, laughing.

He shakes his head and hugs her tight.

'I will treasure your friendship as long as I live, and that will be here, in my world. You must now return to yours.'

She nods and gives him one last squeeze before he waves to us all and sets off to start his life again. Must be *so* weird to be reborn. Like where do you even start, where do you go? Still, that's not our problem.

'So how do we do this, then?' I say. 'How do we get back?'

'Methought you had learned a thing or two in your time here,' Allison says, tucking her chin in and looking like a teacher – she'd be looking over her glasses, if she wore them. 'Is it not obvious?'

Sarah-Jane pats the book, as if to reiterate the point. *Got it.* Looks like the Groveses are back together, and we're singing again. She hands it to me, the embossed cover now covered in Matty's teeth marks, and I open it up on the page that I twig now is Thackeray's doing – dimension-hopping bastard that he was. Sandy and I hold it between us.

Before we start, though, I look at Allison and Sarah-Jane. My friends. 'You two are coming with us, right?'

'Matty, don't be daft. Of course they are, they want out of this bollocks of a patriarchal world – can't you tell?'

Allison and Sarah-Jane grin, and both place their hands on the book. Then we sing – all of us, even the girls. All together, and all in time.

34
Matty

Four of us left Old England, but it's six that end up in the car park outside the Jack-in-the-Green inn. We all shot out of the white light in sequence – it's me and Sandy first, tumbling out and hitting the side of my Traveller that's still parked up, and then Allison and Sarah-Jane. Then two soapy-looking girls fell out, muttering among themselves and pointing at my car with their eyes about to shoot out of their heads.

They light up when they see Sandy and run to give her a group hug.

'Ellyn! Mercy!' She says, her voice cracking. Guess she made some friends of her own. 'What happened?'

'Oh, please, Sandy! After all you had told us of your world… we needed to see it! And when Mercy did espy you all standing with the book, and the white light – we took our chance. We ran and jumped right in lest the light should extinguish.' She stops then and looks at her feet. 'I do hope you mind not?'

'Don't be daft! You're well rid of that place,' Sandy says,

hugging them again. Warmly. I shiver, because it's night now and the wind's got up. Sarah-Jane's examining my car like some geek at a classic car meet, running her hands over the bonnet and peering in through the glass. Allison's spotted the electric light above the pub sign and is in the process of trying to snuff it out, shooting bursts of wind with her wand that make the sign creak, but not touching the light which stays on. I clear my throat.

'There's something we need to sort out,' I announce. All heads turn to me, and it's then, behind Sarah-Jane, that I notice the panda car parked up. I'm not all that pleased about it, because I've still got the memories of sitting in the back of one, which made me promise myself that I'd never deal with the police again if I could bloody well help it.

Sandy grabs my hand and squeezes it tight. She senses my unease.

'Come on then, smart-arse,' she says, grinning. 'Let's see how we're gonna talk our way out of this one.'

She leads the way into the pub, and it's like we never even left. The tables and stools are all overturned, and the hand-painted flyover sign is still up. And up at the bar, Karen's leaning over with her earrings still dangling, only her make-up's run all down her face making her look a bit like a demonic clown. The clothes don't help, or the way she's waving her arms about with her eyes wide, talking to the two police officers standing with pencils scribbling furiously in notepads.

'You say there was a light once they said the words,' the woman officer says, shooting her colleague a look. 'Do you think you could describe it? Was it a flash, or –?'

Karen slaps the bar-top.

'The *light*, God, it was so bright I thought my eyes might burn right out of my head! It was whiter than white, if you know what I mean – it gave you that eye-ache, the kind if you're on a bright computer late at night... Laurence, wouldn't you say?'

Laurence? I'd almost forgotten about the old prick who knew about the book. He'd tried to warn us, telling us not to read from it – I realise that now. He's sitting up at the bar next to the police and staring straight at us. Looking like he wants to laugh his head off.

'You might ask The Groveses themselves, Karen,' he says, and points right at us. Karen shrieks, and totters straight over, nearly going arse over tit over a bar stool.

'Er, miss us?' I ask and feel Sandy's elbow in my ribs.

She puts a hand on my face and Sandy's.

'Where on earth have you been these past two hours? What *happened* to you?'

Two hours? It never really crossed my mind that time might move differently here and there, that days might only be hours. I'm sure Allison will be able to explain it to me some time.

'We... had to pick up some fans,' Sandy says, indicating the Old England girls. *Clever old Sandy.* 'We should have said there'd be an intermission. Sorry.'

'Aye,' Sarah-Jane says, and Allison covers her face with her hands in disbelief as though she knows she's going to say something that'll blow it all. 'I can attest that we wanted to hear the music.'

'But – the earthquake! And the *light*,' Karen says. I feel

for her, I really do, for the sake of being shown up in front of the old bill who've put their notebooks away and are now muttering to each other. 'How do you explain *that*? How do you explain the pair of you disappearing for two hours?'

I shrug, cool as I can manage.

'Told you it'd be a good show, didn't we?'

Sandy nods and looks at the old boy, still smiling ear to ear.

'It's just a folk story – right, Laurence?'

'A curse, supposedly,' he says. 'One I am afraid my own ancestor, Thackeray Rowan, may be responsible for. Never mind all that, I must *apologise*. I'm sorry for filling your heads with such rubbish. Let me buy you all a drink and let's have another song.'

We take our cue from his cheeky little old man wink, and head back over to the makeshift stage. On the way, I make sure to slide the book back into its place on the shelf by the booth – though maybe I should have held onto it as a keepsake, or else burn it to stop any other craziness happening.

Our instruments and gear are still there, and Karen's still talking to the police officers as we re-arrange everything and set up again. It's a bit anti-climactic – almost like we never left, and we really have just had an intermission. The girls have taken it upon themselves to put the tables and stools right, and Allison and Sarah-Jane are deep in conversation with Laurence as he describes all the different drinks and snacks they could have.

'What was the encore gonna be?' I ask Sand, because she might remember our original set list better than me. 'Was it *Tam Lin*?'

She stands the mic stand back up, and picks up her fiddle, checking the tuning.

'Yeah, we'll go with that. Actually, Matty – and I think we should have a proper talk about it – I really do think we should start incorporating more rock into our sets. Honest. I think I've had just about enough Old England to last me a lifetime.'

'And I just about get the appeal, now. I'm sorry for being a prick about it all.'

She ruffles my hair.

'Don't even worry about it, numb-nuts. Let's do what we came here to do.'

Allison and Sarah-Jane have taken seats now, next to Ellyn and Mercy, while Karen and Laurence invite the police to stay and listen at the bar. It's got to be the best audience we've ever had.

I look around, imagining how packed this place was – even the booths were full when we started our set. Even the one by the window, with the bull's eyeglass, had been full. That's a cosy place to sit, with the candle in an old wine bottle, reflecting off the glass. It illuminates the leaves outside.

I don't remember any bushes by the windows. I don't even think there were any flower boxes or anything outside. Sandy's saying some bollocks about the history of *Tam Lin*, but I tune out. There're leaves, and they're moving.

Then the eyes open, under a furrowed leafy brow, and stick-hands rap on the glass. They thunder through the pub, breaking up Sandy's speech, and Sarah-Jane waves to the foliage as Allison rushes to open the window. She gives up with the metal catch and just waves the wand to make the glass disappear, which sends Karen into a meltdown. The head of Jack-in-the-Green pops through, and the police officers follow Karen's lead.

'Groveses!' He doesn't even acknowledge anybody else in the room. 'I fear it does fall upon me to enlist your aid. The fabric is mended, but something throws off the balance of Old England yet. Please, would you find it in your hearts to return with me?'

Sandy looks at me, her eyes full of that human concern and kindness. I look at her, a bit worried myself. And against my better judgement, I sigh.

'Come on, then – let's go.'

The End.

Lightning Source UK Ltd.
Milton Keynes UK
UKHW040845110220
358525UK00001B/58